# CHARACTERS

## ❈ EARNEST FLAMING

The universally feared "Empress" and de facto boss of the school. Hard on herself, and on everyone else, too. A top student, she is gifted in both academics and practical skills, and even the school's teachers bow to her will. She is the daughter of a prestigious noble family and the possessor of a sword imbued with flame magic, to which there may be more than meets the eye...

## ❈ BLADE

A former Hero who defeated the Overlord and restored peace to the world. While he has lost his special Hero powers, even his base strength far surpasses the rest of the student body. His dream is to live out life as a normal person, but people still treat him as an all-powerful super being.

# SOPHITIA FEMTO

The number-two student at the academy after Earnest, also known as the "Ice Queen." A cool beauty who is impassive, unmoved, and indifferent no matter what the subject. Nonetheless, Blade has piqued her interest. Her mysterious origins may hold an important secret...

# CÚ CHULAINN

A baby dragon who has taken on human form. From the moment she was born, she had never met anyone stronger than her, but then Blade came along and did her in with a single punch. Now she has fully imprinted on him, calling him her "honored Father" and following him wherever he goes.

CLASSROOM FOR HEROES

# CONTENTS

**Chapter 1**
**Earnest**
*001*

**Chapter 2**
**Sophie**
*071*

**Chapter 3**
**Cú Chulainn**
*119*

**Epilogue**
*181*

**Afterword**
*183*

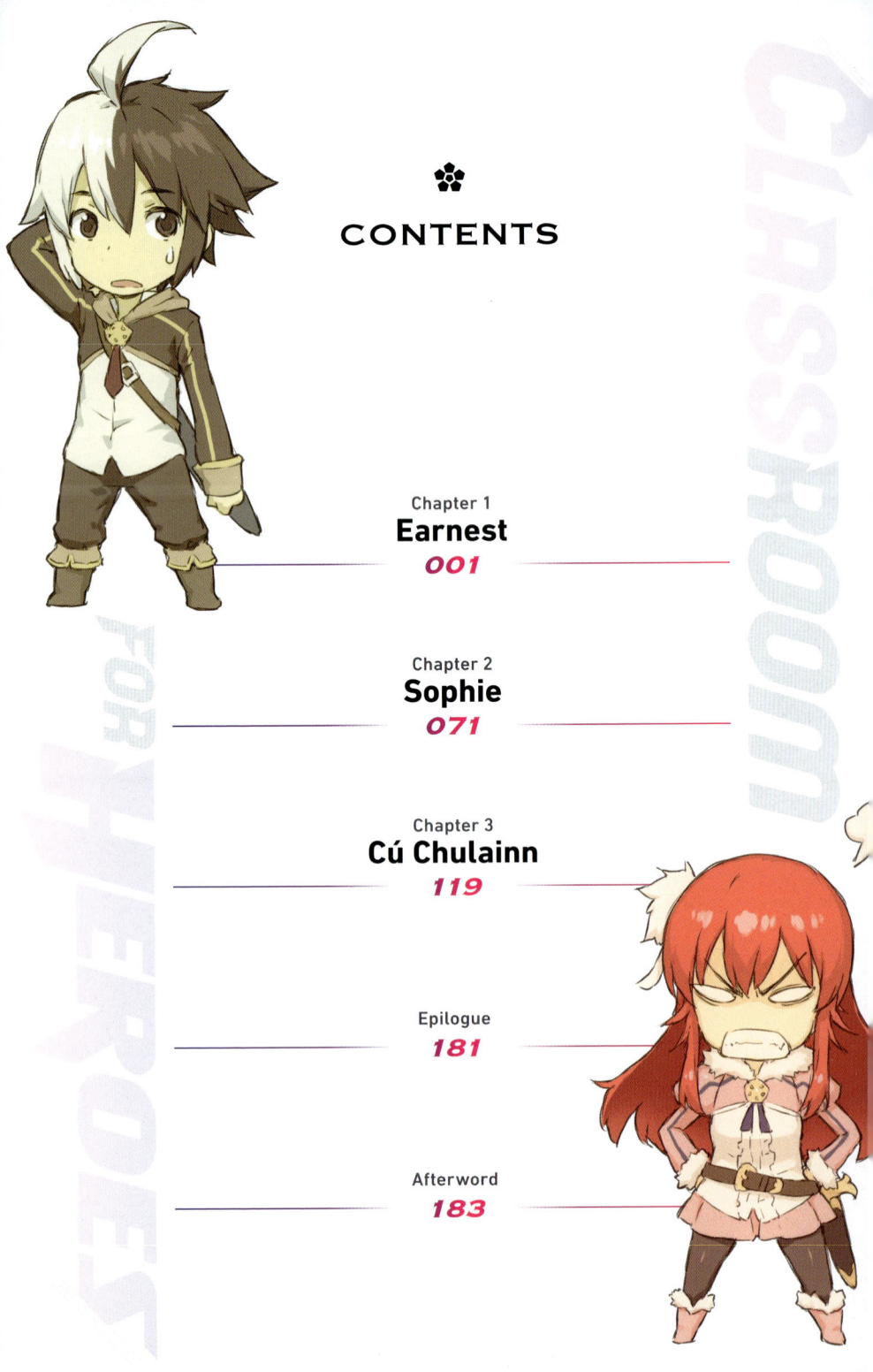

# CLASSROOM FOR HEROES

**Shin Araki**

Illustration by
**Haruyuki Morisawa**

New York

# SHIN ARAKI

**Translation by Kevin Gifford**
**Cover art by Haruyuki Morisawa**

This book is a work of fiction. Names, characters, places, and incidents are the product of the author's imagination or are used fictitiously. Any resemblance to actual events, locales, or persons, living or dead, is coincidental.

EIYU KYOSHITSU © 2015 by Shin Araki
All rights reserved.
Illustration by Haruyuki Morisawa.
First published in Japan in 2015 by SHUEISHA, Inc. English translation rights arranged with SHUEISHA, Inc. through Tuttle-Mori Agency, Inc., Tokyo.

English translation © 2024 by Yen Press, LLC

Yen Press, LLC supports the right to free expression and the value of copyright. The purpose of copyright is to encourage writers and artists to produce the creative works that enrich our culture.

The scanning, uploading, and distribution of this book without permission is a theft of the author's intellectual property. If you would like permission to use material from the book (other than for review purposes), please contact the publisher. Thank you for your support of the author's rights.

Yen On
150 West 30th Street, 19th Floor
New York, NY 10001

Visit us at yenpress.com • facebook.com/yenpress • twitter.com/yenpress
yenpress.tumblr.com • instagram.com/yenpress

First Yen On Edition: March 2024
Edited by Yen On Editorial: Emma McClain
Designed by Yen Press Design: Eddy Mingki

Yen On is an imprint of Yen Press, LLC.
The Yen On name and logo are trademarks of Yen Press, LLC.

The publisher is not responsible for websites (or their content) that are not owned by the publisher.

Library of Congress Cataloging-in-Publication Data
Names: Araki, Shin, 1968– author. | Morisawa, Haruyuki, illustrator. | Gifford, Kevin, translator.
Title: Classroom for heroes / Shin Araki ; illustration by Haruyuki Morisawa ; translation by Kevin Gifford.
Description: First Yen On edition. | New York, NY : Yen On, 2024–
Identifiers: LCCN 2023055524 | ISBN 9781975378684 (v. 1 ; trade paperback) | ISBN 9781975378707 (v. 2 ; trade paperback) | ISBN 9781975378721 (v. 3 ; trade paperback) | ISBN 9781975378745 (v. 4 ; trade paperback) | ISBN 9781975378769 (v. 5 ; trade paperback) | ISBN 9781975378783 (v. 6 ; trade paperback)
Subjects: CYAC: Fantasy. | Schools—Fiction. | Heroes—Fiction. |
LCGFT: Fantasy fiction. | Light novels.
Classification: LCC PZ7.1.A7216 Cl 2024 | DDC [Fic]— dc23
LC record available at https://lccn.loc.gov/2023055524

ISBNs: 978-1-9753-7868-4 (paperback)
978-1-9753-7869-1 (ebook)

10 9 8 7 6 5 4 3 2 1

LSC-C

Printed in the United States of America

# Classroom for Heroes

### Shin Araki
Illustration by
**Haruyuki Morisawa**

## Chapter 1:
# Earnest

○ **Scene I: Hallway, Lunch Break**

The hallway was full of the hustle and bustle you'd expect during lunch break, and one young man, wearing the same uniform as everyone else, was standing stationary in the middle of it. Students walked around him as he remained frozen in place. Frankly, he was seriously getting in the way of traffic…and he didn't even seem to notice.

*Yes! It's happening! Nobody's looking at me! I'm not standing out in any way!*

He was too busy letting his emotions get the better of him, his hands balled into tight fists.

It wasn't that nobody was looking at him; they were just avoiding eye contact because he was acting so suspiciously—but he wasn't making that distinction in his mind. He might've seen what was happening as "not standing out," but the truth was he couldn't have stood out more if he tried. He simply refused to notice. At all.

*I've done it! I've finally done it! At long last, I'm finally a* normal *person!*

He balled up his fists even tighter, emphasizing the word *normal* in his mind. Being normal was key, since people used to call him a "super-being."

*An overwhelming sense of normalcy is washing over me! I'm so incredibly normal it hurts!*

His name was Blade, and after various events, he had transferred into this school.

*Ahhh... Being normal is so wonderful. I love not standing out. All hail averageness!*

With an almost audible *zing*, he gave the students around him a sneer from the depths of his very being. The ones exposed to it rushed past, assuming he was trying to catch their attention. But that wasn't the case—he was just so excited that he couldn't help putting his entire soul into his eyes. He was trying to act natural and blend in with all the normal students around him, but instead he was just standing out more than ever. And yet...as expected, that fact never dawned on Blade.

But there was a group of four curiously watching him instead of running for their lives. That group consisted of two girls and two boys, all of whom took an interest in the shady character named Blade, watching him from afar with fascination.

Blade noticed them as well. And the moment he did, he began stomping toward them. His eyes, brimming with excitement, gave the quartet the impression that he was coming over to stab them all to death. The most weak willed among them let out a tiny "Eep" of horror as she tried not to cry; even the boys reared back a little.

*This is it. My first step as a normal person! Time to say hello!*

Blade briskly raised a hand. "Hey!" he said loudly. "I'm the He—um, I mean, I am Blade!"

He quickly corrected himself before he could reveal his true identity.

"Uh...yeah, n-nice to meet you..."

The first to react, despite the tears in her eyes, was a girl with long, dark hair. She seemed timid, but there was more than a hint of kindness on her face. Her name was Claire, and she was from the junior class.

"I am Blade!" the boy said once again, each word brimming with energy.

Claire blinked a few times. "Huh?"

"I am Blade!" he said a third time, his face as carefree as a young child's.

"Um...okay. I... My name's Claire."

"Claire? Wow!"

His face lit up. He grinned, seemingly filled with joy at the new piece of information. His childlike glee caused Claire to smile a little in return.

Blade kept beaming—he was acting like he had just made his first friend ever. In fact, that was completely true. At least, she was his first friend anywhere close to him in age.

He turned toward the other three, hope shining on his face.

"My name is Yessica," said the other girl among them. She had shorter hair and looked sensible and put together. The boys followed suit.

"Clayde."

"My name's Kassim."

"I am Blade!" came the boy's answer. He couldn't have looked happier.

"You already said that."

"You're a funny guy."

The four of them smiled and laughed—a generally favorable reaction. The alarm they had felt was now firmly in the past.

Meanwhile, Blade was cheering internally. *I've made four whole friends! Now it's official! No matter how you slice it, I'm completely, perfectly normal!*

But then a thought occurred to him, and he stopped.

*Wait. Don't people normally have more friends than this? Maybe four isn't enough to make me normal. No, it can't be. I need a lot more. B-but how many...? Ten? Would having ten be normal? No, wait, don't jump to conclusions. How about...a hundred? Can I be normal once I befriend a hundred people? Would that work?*

It was a profound question, and it troubled Blade mightily.

"What are you people doing over there?"

The four students facing him immediately turned toward the voice and winced. Blade followed their gazes, spinning around a few seconds after them.

A girl was standing in front of them with her arms crossed. With her blazing-red hair and red outfit, she looked like a student to be reckoned with. In this hallway where every other student was wearing an identical uniform, she alone was different. Her gaze was sharp and merciless as she glared at Blade and the four others standing with him in the hallway.

This was Earnest Flaming, class president and the most feared student in the school.

"Oh crap," Yessica said, "it's the Empress." She clearly intended for Earnest to hear her, and judging by the way the other girl's face had twitched just now, the attempt had succeeded. But Earnest didn't say anything more.

Blade was befuddled. "The Emp…?" he whispered, unsure what this meant.

"You are all standing in the middle of the hallway," said the girl. "You're blocking traffic. Think about all the trouble you're causing everyone. If you see yourself as students of this glorious academy, you must always strive to follow the rules and protect the order of…"

She began to lecture them. They were all the same age, but there was clearly a gap between the regular student body and Empress Earnest Flaming—one just as wide as, if not wider than, that between teacher and student. In fact, even the school's teachers were subject to this girl's lectures.

…But none of it worked on Blade. He didn't know, after all, just how scary this young girl could be. But more than that, as he was a former superbeing, it would take an Ancient Dragon, or a magic beast of equal or higher rank, to even begin to scare him. None of the "mere" people walking around this town could possibly arouse such feelings.

So Blade simply stared dully at Earnest as she griped at the group of four by his side.

*She's…not a teacher, right? She's a student, even though she's not in uniform.*

In fact, Earnest was lecturing Blade as well, but he didn't see it that way. All the while, he was thinking, *Why are Claire and her friends getting yelled at like this?*

But as he stared at Earnest and leisurely pondered the situation, he had a sudden realization.

"Ohhh! Right! I needed to go to the chancellor's office!"

His near-hysteric voice stopped Earnest's lecture in its tracks. Her eyes swiveled almost audibly, settling on him.

"And you're...who? I haven't seen you before."

Claire lifted her index finger slightly. "Um, uh, Lady Earnest..."

"*No.* Not 'Lady.' Do not call me that."

"Okay! ...Um, I think Blade's a new transfer student!"

"A transfer student? Joining this glorious school in the middle of the semester? That's unheard of—"

"Listen," interrupted Blade, "I need to go to the chancellor's office right now!"

He repeated himself, presumably because he thought nobody had heard him the first time. After he cut her off again, Earnest glared at him, her eyes practically boring holes in his face. But even exposure to this potentially lethal stare elicited no reaction from Blade. He stood there blithely, unaffected. The other four, watching from the side, were growing noticeably pale. Anyone who belonged to this school—the students, of course, but the teachers, too—knew that the Empress's withering gaze was something to avoid at all costs. But it failed to work on Blade. In fact, it seemed doubtful that he even realized she was glaring at him.

The four of them turned toward Blade with looks of astonished respect.

"Oh, right. Can you show me the way to the chancellor's office?"

Blade was talking to the *Empress*, of all people. "Why would I do that?!" she shot back, not disguising the wrath in her voice as she stared daggers at him. This combined package would have murdered anyone else. Twice.

"What, you don't know where it is?" Blade asked.

"*Yes*, I *do!!*" she replied, taking the bait. And with that, she was now socially obligated to show him the way. The four onlookers stared wide-eyed as the pair left together.

## ○ Scene II: Corridor

The two of them were walking down a deserted corridor.

Earnest was taking the lead, throwing out her chest, striding forward, eyes focused only on what lay ahead. Her gait betrayed more than a hint of indignation.

Blade followed, his arms crossed behind his head and his eyes darting around, taking in their surroundings. This was his first time at the academy, and everything was a rare and novel sight to him. The main school was housed in a stately stone building, and the view from the long, covered outdoor passageways was resplendent with nature's greenery.

Ivy grew along the handrails. Blade spotted a dragonfly perched on one of the leaves. He reached out to it.

"What are you doing?" asked Earnest.

"Huh? Oh, I'll release it."

He opened his hand and let go of the insect. It flew off, its wings uninjured.

Earnest squinted, giving Blade the most dubious look she could muster. She had turned back because he was no longer following…only to find him playing with bugs?!

She spun around in a huff and quickly began walking again. It was the first time in her life that someone had disrespected her like this. She was a noble by birth, and she considered it normal for anyone she met to already know who she was.

And now she'd been forced to serve as a *guide*…?

She pressed on, burning with resentment.

They arrived at the door to the chancellor's office. Blade could tell because the word CHANCELLOR was written on it.

With a brisk snapping of her wrist, Earnest knocked three times, then called out without bothering to wait.

"Excuse me, sir! This is Earnest Flaming. I found a lost kid about to cry, so I brought him here."

Blade looked at her in confusion. Finally managing to elicit a reaction out of the boy gave Earnest a tiny sense of vindication. But Blade wasn't taken aback by her venom; he was simply surprised to suddenly hear her speaking so politely.

"Come in," said a voice from inside. Earnest looked puzzled for a moment, but she opened the door and entered—and the moment she saw who was there, her expression visibly changed and her eyes went wide.

Blade stepped around Earnest, who was now blocking the entrance, and went into the room. "Yo," he said. "I'm here."

"Wha— You *fool*!" she cried. "Do you have any…any *idea* who this person is?!"

Earnest confronted Blade, angrier than ever. Then she glanced back at the other person in the room. He was a robust-looking man in the prime of life. It was His Majesty the King, the most famous person in the kingdom, renowned as the Lion Monarch.

"Sure I do," Blade replied casually. This earned him another glare from Earnest, who then turned back toward the king, facing him head-on.

"Why are you here in the chancellor's office…Your Majesty?"

She was perfectly polite, the exact opposite of a few moments ago. Even the Empress of this academy was reduced to a kitten before the king.

"Yes… A good question," the king placidly replied from his chair.

"Thank you, sire. I am honored by your presence."

Earnest straightened up even more as the king addressed her. She was blushing. Even for a daughter of nobility, the king was a truly lofty presence. She might catch sight of him at a state ball or the like, but the idea of having an exchange with him was like an impossible dream.

"Earnest Flaming… The *previous* chancellor told me about you. I hear you are quite an exceptional pupil."

"Oh, no, sire, um… I still have very far to go."

Blade was beyond shocked as he studied the face of the girl next to him. All that arrogance of a moment ago had given way to an utterly different person. No, she was like a whole different species.

"Uhm…are *you* going to be the next chancellor, Your Majesty?" Earnest asked.

"Mmm. You truly *are* an excellent talent. You're correct."

"But that…"

Earnest, her face still that of someone else, looked back down. The king of this nation was in the chancellor's office, seated at its main desk. That was enough for Earnest to surmise that His Majesty had taken over the position of chancellor. And now the king, in his new position, had called her "excellent."

"Um..."

She raised her head. With admiration rather than indignation written on her face, she truly looked like a different girl.

"I am certainly aware, sire, of your exploits in the field of battle! It would be a great honor to receive your instruction! Our previous chancellor, you see, was a tad inept in that department."

She blushed as she spoke, boldly working an insult into her remark. Blade winced. Never mind! She was exactly the same species as before.

"Ah, yes," the king replied, keeping the serene smile on his face. "Well, that is all, so..."

"Pardon me, sire?" Earnest replied, smiling back. The sheer glory of conversing with the king made her yearn for even one more second of the wondrous experience.

The king kept on smiling.

"You may go. I need to discuss matters with him."

"Uh...?"

For a moment, Earnest looked like she had no idea what he meant. But as fast as her mind worked, it took less than a second for understanding to spread across her beautiful visage. She then turned to Blade, unleashing her most powerful glare of the day, before silently leaving the room.

## ○ Scene III: The King

The moment the door shut behind her—

"*You're* the reason she's glaring at me, you know."

Blade's tone couldn't have been ruder as he addressed the king.

"Whatever do you mean?"

"Don't give me that," he replied to the man's feigned ignorance.

Hearing Blade speak to him so casually didn't faze the monarch at all. As their interactions indicated, they were old friends. The king shooing everyone else out of a room so he could speak with Blade, and all those other people glaring at Blade as they filed out, had happened dozens of times in the past. *Dozens.*

They had known each other since Blade was an active Hero. The king had backed him and provided support when he was still only a young boy.

"Why school anyway?" asked Blade.

"Don't like it?"

"It's...not that, just..."

Blade paused. It frustrated him that, once again, he'd been made to go along with the king's schemes... But oh well. He had made four friends. And if you counted *her*, the total was now five.

A bit of childlike glee crossed Blade's face for a moment. The king saw this and said, "You know what I want, Blade?"

He sank deeper into his chancellor's chair. It was a luxurious piece of furniture, but it still creaked under the weight of his finely chiseled body.

"...I want you to get your Hero powers back."

"But I want to be a normal person! I want to be *average*!"

Blade raised his voice despite himself. This guy, the king...he just didn't get it. Blade had defeated the Overlord. He'd carried out his duties as a Hero...and then he'd lost his powers. He saw no reason why he should delay the dream he had held for over ten years any longer.

"I think this school will serve as a good means of rehabilitation. The students are all top-tier, you know. They could be just the stimulation you need."

"Listen here, old man..."

"And I think I've shaken up the curriculum quite a bit. I've examined the previous chancellor's approach to education extensively, and if you ask me, he's been a bit too lax. The way things stand, we'll only produce run-of-the-mill champions, at best. To raise a *true* Hero—"

"We don't *need* Heroes anymore, do we? There's no Overlord left."

Besides, thought Blade, Heroes weren't the sort of thing you could create with the right education. People didn't *become* Heroes; they were *born* Heroes.

"Ha-ha! You *did* defeat him, yes." The king roared with laughter.

*...No I didn't. We both lost.*

Blade scowled and turned his back on the king. This old man... Blade couldn't bring himself to hate the guy, but he sure knew how to laugh off anything inconvenient. It was like his special ability—a talent people called charisma. And that, of course, was why he'd been able to unite every country on the continent.

"When you and the Overlord struck each other down, it simultaneously extinguished both the power of the Hero and that of the Overlord. That is how it was explained to me, at least."

"Yeah, 'cause it's true." Blade puffed out his chest. That was why he was now a normal person. He could only do normal stuff—the kinds of things run-of-the-mill champions could.

"Well, *I*, for one, don't believe that," said the king.

"Look..."

"Because you are a *Hero*!" The king's eyes went wide, and veins appeared on his forehead as he bellowed at the top of his lungs.

"This is pointless," Blade said, giving up. The king had always been like this.

"But don't mind me," the man continued. His excitement had vanished, and he'd reassumed his previous, calm demeanor. "Have fun while you're here, won't you? Think of it as a vacation."

When he spoke like this, the king truly felt like a man of character. But Blade knew the truth. Deep down, he was totally different.

Blade chuckled helplessly to himself. At this point, there was nothing he could do but go along with the man's antics.

## ○ Scene IV: Junior Class (Lecture)

Blade had been assigned to the junior class, which used one of the school's lecture halls. In fact, he was there right now, one of many students sitting and listening to the teacher's lecture. The hall was shaped like a large bowl, with the professor at the deepest part of it, droning on in front of a blackboard.

This hall had a sign reading Rank C at the entrance, and it was indeed a Rank C lecture taking place inside. Blade had heard that around a hundred students in total attended this school. Ranks B and C, to which most of the students belonged, were called the "junior class." Rank A was the "senior class," home to the school's elites; only a dozen or so students were in it.

Blade listened to the lecture, already feeling bored.

"And so, as you can see, a flame-driven attack would do little against a Salamander-type monster..."

He yawned. This whole lecture, as he saw it, was just common sense. From what he'd heard, "schools" were supposed to teach you things you didn't know... And yet he hadn't learned anything new from this lesson.

Seated a few rows down was the group of four he had made friends with earlier—Claire, Yessica, Clayde, and Kassim. As his gaze casually drifted their way, Yessica turned around and gave him a friendly wave hello. Blade waved back. Claire, seated next to Yessica, mumbled a warning to her, something like "Don't do that." Blade chuckled.

The teacher continued enthusiastically.

"...Now, an effective method for handling this was discovered by the Earl of Jäger in 1715 AH..."

Blade let out a big yawn, and a brilliant idea occurred to him. He used a marker to draw eyes on his eyelids, disguising himself as he fell asleep in his seat. Clayde, a handsome but straitlaced kind of guy, found this hilarious. It took everything he had to keep from laughing out loud. But Blade was too busy sleeping to notice.

✱

"Oh?"

As he graded quizzes after class, the professor's eyes stopped on a certain answer sheet. The name "Blade" was written on it, and when he reviewed it...

"Hmm. Perfect."

This student, it seemed, had no reason to stay in his class. The professor took out another sheet of paper—a recommendation for promotion to the next rank—and signed his name.

## ○ Scene V: Junior Class (Practical)

This school took a dual-pronged approach to education, valuing the literary and military arts in equal measure. Students' time was evenly divided between sit-down lectures and practical study, and right now a group of several dozen B- and C-ranked junior students were seated in a circle on the Proving Ground, the school's main training arena. A military instructor stood in the middle, staging a little performance.

*Thwap!*

With a satisfying sound, a sword sliced a suit of armor in two. A round of applause and cheering erupted from the students as the instructor sheathed his weapon with an equally satisfying *shiiing*.

"Put in the right training, and in no time at all, *you* will be doing this, too."

"Whaaat?" came the students' dubious reply.

"Now get out there!"

He pointed an arm toward a row of neatly arranged, identical suits of armor. Each one was placed on a pedestal, waiting to be cleaved apart. The students gingerly approached the weapon racks, then picked out their swords and headed over to the armor.

Looking at how they held their blades, they weren't complete amateurs. Each of them appeared to have a decent amount of experience. But when faced with the suits of armor, they all seemed hesitant to make any bold moves. They furtively looked around, checking to see if anyone would step up first...

"I'll do it."

The speaker was one of Blade's friends—Clayde, that good-looking swordsman. He glared hard at the armor, expertly maintaining his battle stance. He stayed still for a few moments, and then—

*"Haaah!"*

—shouting, he slashed at his target. With a sharp *claaang*, his sword dug about halfway through the armor, then stopped cold.

"Ugh... It's too solid..." he muttered to himself as he pried his blade out. It had clear nicks up and down the length of it.

"Hey, Blade! You gonna try, or...?"

"Hmm?"

Blade turned toward the voice and found Claire. She had a sword in her hands, but her grip seemed strange.

"I, um, I'm not very good with, with swords," she said, fidgeting. "I'm good at bludgeoning things to death, but..."

*Aha*, thought Blade. Her grip and stance were the right approach if she was wielding a mace. But unlike with a weapon that relied mainly on heft, with a sword, it was important to keep the alignment of the blade in mind, or else it'd be tough to hew much of anything.

"So you gonna try?" she said again.

"Hmm..."

At the look of anticipation on Claire's face, Blade hesitated. He thought for a bit, tapping his shoulder with the sword he normally carried on his back. He wasn't trying to work out a way to slice through the armor, however. He was pondering how *not* to slice.

*They want me to cut through only the armor, right? That's gonna be kinda hard...*

Indeed, doing exactly as the instructor demonstrated would be a little difficult. *He* had slashed through only the armor; the pedestal hadn't been torn to splinters. That struck Blade as pretty—well, *extremely*—tough to duplicate. In actual battle, after all, there was no need for showy, nimble moves like slicing through *only* a suit of armor. Blade, at least, had never tried it. In *his* line of work, as long as he bisected the occupant of the armor as well, nobody had any complaints.

"Well, guess I'll give it a try," he said at last.

"Yeah! You really should!"

Cheered on by Claire, Blade turned toward the armor. *Keep it small*, he whispered to himself. *Small.*

"Oof."

With a light, easy motion, he swung his sword.

"Ahhhh!"

Screams were followed by a roaring noise. Then came the shock wave.

The pedestal supporting the armor was completely subsumed. Claire's skirt was blown upward, flapping in the intense wind, revealing the full, brazen glory of her lily-white undergarments.

When the wind died down at last, the armor was unrecognizable. The pedestal had been split in two by the shock wave. Even the ground had been gouged out beneath it.

"Right! There we go!"

Blade nodded to himself, satisfied with his work. He had kept the local damage to a minimum. He had sliced only the armor…or rather, he'd *destroyed* only the armor. "Cutting" didn't really do justice to what had happened… Still, a decent effort. Eight out of ten, maybe.

"I *did* it!"

He turned toward Claire in triumph. She was still holding her skirt down, and next to her stood everyone else, looking on in blank amazement. Even the instructor had his mouth half-open as he stared at Blade.

*Huh…? Wait, did I…mess up, maybe?*

A single streak of cold sweat ran down Blade's forehead.

## ○ Scene VI: To the Senior Class

A few days later, Blade was walking down the hall toward his next afternoon class. He had been ordered during lunch break that day to begin reporting to the senior class, and he was headed for his first lecture.

He was wearing a necklace with a little plate reading RANK A on it. Flipping it over, he saw that it contained a grid of small squares, meant to be stamped by his teachers. Once a student earned enough stamps, they'd receive a class upgrade.

He'd risen through the ranks with unprecedented speed, but to Blade, this was neither an honor nor a privilege. His only thought was *Gee, it sucks that I'm being separated from the friends I just made...*

"The senior class, huh?" He fiddled with the plate dangling from his neck as he muttered to himself.

Ranks B and C, the junior class, shared some lectures, but the seniors in Rank A had a wholly independent curriculum. He recalled the faces of his four friends as they saw him off. Claire and the others all smiled and waved, promising to join him soon.

Could he make friends in the senior class, too? He kept walking, filled with anticipation and just a little bit of anxiety.

The moment he reached the Proving Ground, Blade realized how different the atmosphere was from the junior class.

First, there weren't as many people. Before, he'd always had tons of students clamoring around him, but now the area was nearly empty. The entire class consisted of a dozen or so students.

Next, nobody here was wearing a school uniform. They all got to choose their own outfits, and they were so colorful, he bet he could find every hue in the rainbow if he looked hard enough. Blade had grown accustomed to the monochrome uniforms, and he felt it would take his eyes a while to adjust to this new scenery.

One more thing: Several students immediately spun around whenever Blade looked at them, like they had eyes in the back of their heads. Of those, he stared hard at one girl in particular. She was the "blue" member of this colorful troupe, sporting a blue cape and partially hiding her lips with a blue scarf. Her face was expressionless, and while she had stopped looking at Blade a while ago, he couldn't help observing her. Not that he was super curious about her or anything. It was just one of those idiosyncrasies you adopted as a Hero—or rather, an ex-Hero. If someone looked like a tested fighter, Blade couldn't keep his eyes from wandering over to them.

The next person he took an interest in was a girl clad entirely in red…

*Hang on a minute.*

"That red girl…"

He remembered her. And as he stared at her impertinently, it became clear she remembered him, too. Her face, already scary, grew even more peeved. She immediately stormed across the Proving Ground arena, stomping angrily as she made her way toward him.

"Why are *you* in the senior class?!" she asked menacingly, demanding an explanation. This was Earnest Flaming, someone whose name Blade had memorized back on the day of his transfer.

"Oh, um, I'm in this class starting today."

He picked up the plate hanging at his chest and showed it to her. She grabbed it, all but seizing it from him, then flipped it over.

"*Ughhh…*"

She was pulling on it so hard that Blade began to choke.

"Instructor Grateau, Instructor Morrigan, even Instructor Thane… I can't believe it. You bribed Instructor *Aster*, too?!"

"Bribed?"

"Of course," she said arrogantly. "There's no way you went from C to A in just a few days."

"Well, I kinda did."

"And *besides*…" Earnest placed a hand on her curvy hip. "This is an honorable academy with a long history. One only the truly strong may attend. Someone as sloppy, slapdash, and unmotivated as *you* could never be admitted here. All this, just because His Majesty recommended you… I don't know what kind of trickery you used, but mark my words, I will expose it to the world!"

*The king's the one resorting to trickery, actually. And I'd be over the moon if she could expose him for me. If she could punish him, too, that'd be even better.*

As Blade listened to Earnest, he realized that her problem with him mainly had to do with his perceived lack of enthusiasm.

"Hey, I'm motivated," he said.

"What? How?"

"I wanna make friends."

"Huh?"

Blade was a normal person now, and so he wanted to make a hundred friends. That was his dream.

"C'mon, introduce me to some people," he continued.

He glanced around the arena. There were a dozen or so people in the senior class, and all of them looked *interesting*, to say the least. But Earnest saw Blade's attitude as insincere, and it riled her. He saw her begin to shake, just before she totally lost her temper.

"*Listen to me!*" she shouted, rage flowing from every pore. "I'm *trying* to pick a fight with you!"

Finally, she was being honest. She'd just admitted that what she wanted was to get up in his business and goad him into snapping back at her. So she was aware of it.

"Yeah, I'm listening."

As Blade took in his surroundings, he placed a hand on Earnest's head. This made her turn even redder. She hadn't been patted on the head since she was five.

"Don't *pet* me!"

She drew her sword and swiped at him with her full strength. Blade leaned to one side to dodge its trajectory. For him, it was a completely unconscious movement. He hadn't even noticed that she had attacked him, much less that he had evaded it.

"Huh? Who's that?"

His eyes were focused somewhere faraway. There, standing ahead of him, was the blue-clothed girl from before.

"Which one?" Earnest asked, fixing her hair. Between Blade's hand and her potentially lethal slash, the bun she normally pulled her hair back into had come apart—and the idea of people seeing her with her hair down embarrassed her.

Meticulously fixing her hair, Earnest asked again, "Who do you mean?"

"Her! The blue girl."

"Oh… That's Sophie."

Sophie, apparently sensing their gazes, glanced back at them.

"She sure is strong."

"Well, she's certainly not *weak*. She's in the senior class, after all."

Earnest's face reddened a bit, and she seemed a tad self-conscious as she spoke. Her hair was all back in place now, and she resumed her usual scowl. She had redonned her mask.

"I want to make friends in this class, too. I need a second one!"

Blade was back to badgering her. He seemed almost like a child.

"Your second? Who in the world is your first?"

Earnest looked puzzled. There was no way anyone here could be friends with this cheating, back-door-using alleged "student" of—

"You," Blade said, pointing at a spot around Earnest's chest.

"Wha—? What? *What?!*" She put both hands up in a protective pose as she stammered. "…What do you mean, *me*?!" she asked, face reddening.

"Well, I know your name."

"Huh? What are you, *stupid*?"

Earnest was astounded. This idiot thought knowing her name meant they were friends?

"Oh, right—thanks for guiding me to the chancellor's office. I forgot to thank you earlier."

"W-well, that was no big deal— Wait, no! Never mind that! Do you have some kind of death wish?!"

Before their squabbling could degenerate any further, someone approached. They both turned to see Sophie standing right beside them.

"Earnest… New recruit… The instructor's calling for us to assemble."

Until they heard Sophie's quiet voice, neither of them had noticed her presence at all. Earnest stopped cold, looking embarrassed like she'd made a mistake. She had grown so distracted by her fight with Blade that she had let someone approach her without realizing. She only had herself to blame. In contrast to her shame, Blade looked genuinely impressed.

"I am Blade!" he said, greeting Sophie with a bright, carefree smile. It was the exact same thing he had said to Claire, Yessica, Clayde, and Kassim in the junior class.

"……"

Sophie met his greeting with silence. She seemed nonplussed as she looked back at him.

"I am Blade!" he repeated, just as before.

"He wants your name," interjected Earnest. She was afraid he might repeat the greeting indefinitely if she didn't intervene.

"Is that an order?" Sophie asked with complete seriousness.

"This is kind of how she is," Earnest explained to Blade.

"I am Blade!"

But the boy wasn't giving up. Earnest, however, was ready to throw in the towel. She had seen enough.

"…Sophie."

The light, whisper-like sound came from behind the girl's scarf. Earnest looked back at her, shocked. It was the first time she had seen Sophie do anything without being ordered.

"Sophie! Great! I am Blade! Nice to meet you!"

Blade reached out with one hand. Sophie looked at it blankly. Apparently, a handshake was going too far. Or more likely, she didn't even know what the gesture meant.

"Hey!" shouted another classmate. "We gotta assemble!"

At that, Blade, Earnest, and Sophie walked toward the instructor.

## ○ Scene VII: Examination

All the members of the senior class stood in a line. Blade was among them, still looking left, right, behind, and in front of him. It was quite the rogues' gallery. The junior class students all appeared pretty mature—glad to be here and dedicated to their education—but those in the senior class seemed truly fascinating. The guy who had just called Blade and Earnest over was now standing next to him, and he was a total hunk with long blond hair and his shirt mysteriously unbuttoned, exposing fully half of his upper body. Blade didn't have a clear standard for other people's personal beauty, but he was pretty sure this guy fell into the "heartthrob" category.

Blade squirmed. He *really* wanted to be friends with him.

The instructor was facing the line of students, and Earnest, for some reason, was standing next to him.

"Instructor," she said, "I'd like to put our new recruit through an examination." She was speaking to the instructor, but she wasn't looking at him. Her eyes were focused on Blade instead, drilling into him. Blade, however, didn't realize she was glaring at him. His only thought was *Why does she keep looking at me?*

"Well, you know, our curriculum for today, you see...," the instructor mumbled to the side of Earnest's face. But she wasn't about to accept so weak a protest.

"I'm sure you won't mind," she said.

"N-no, but um..."

Earnest, annoyed, turned to the instructor and delivered a single, piercing glance.

"Oh...all right," the instructor said, looking down at the ground dejectedly.

"What do you want me to do?" Blade asked.

He addressed his question to the boss of this arena, and that was clearly Earnest. He was aware enough to realize that when she'd said "Our new recruit," she'd meant him. He tapped his shoulder with the blade in his hands. He had already picked a sword from the rack. It was a standard-issue type, nothing famous or magical, but having one in hand always helped him calm down. He was a little envious of how Earnest got to carry one around at all times...but he knew that normal people didn't do that. He had quit the Hero business and become a normal person, so it'd be crazy for him to go around packing a weapon. Thus, he only used swords during practice sessions like this one.

"Anything you want. So long as it demonstrates your training."

"Anything, huh?" Blade casually accepted the challenge.

Turning around, he found ten or so sets of armor lined up behind him. Each had been affixed to a pedestal, presumably set up by the instructor for the day's class. In the junior class, they had used plain old suits of metal armor. With the right technique, anyone could use a metal sword to cut through them. But in the senior class, they weren't playing around with mere metal.

"That's magic metal, isn't it?" he said.

"Is there something wrong with that?" Earnest sniffed, a hint of arrogance in her voice. Slicing through magic metal with a nonmagic blade was unheard of. It'd be like trying to cut metal with a wooden sword. To pull it off, you'd need something beyond mere muscle or technique.

*Hmm...*

Blade readied his sword.

"And you know, if it's just cutting through that, *anyone* in this class can do it. So prove to them you belong here. And if you don't...you know the consequences, don't you?"

"Y-yes, defy the Empress and she'll send you flying...," said the instructor weakly. Was that supposed to be advice?

Earnest glared at Blade, challenging him with her eyes. Inside, her anger at Blade's "trickery" still raged. As far as she was concerned, Blade had lied and cheated his way into this school. The king she loved and respected was showing him preferential treatment, and she couldn't stand for it. Forcing him to prove his worth in public like this would expose the whole charade for good—and Earnest couldn't wait to see it happen.

"This *is* the senior class," she advised. "It's dimensions away from the junior class."

She'd heard that he caused some sort of commotion back in the junior class. Probably some kind of cheap, flashy trick devised to hoodwink his peers. *But that was junior level. If he thinks he can shock the seniors, too… well, let's see him try.*

"Huh," said Blade. "Dimensions? …How many?"

"What?" The strange question flustered Earnest.

"Like, how many dimensions?"

"Um, two…? No! Wait! Three! It's three whole dimensions away!" she said boastfully—chest out, hand on one hip, acting as big as possible. She'd padded the numbers a bit.

"Oh… Three, huh…?"

Blade thought for a moment. In the junior class, he'd scared everyone half to death with his overpowered strike. He couldn't repeat that mistake. Perhaps he had misjudged his performance last time by a dimension or so. And if the seniors were three dimensions away, he'd need to go two above what he tried back then…

…So was it okay if he was a bit more serious this time? Ever since that incident, he had been on tiptoe, taking extreme care with everything he did. It was frankly starting to stress him out. But if the senior class was three dimensions away, that *should* mean he could let loose a little.

With a smile on his lips, Blade assumed his battle stance.

*"Haaaaaaah…"*

His body filled with power. But he wasn't just tensing his muscles—he was summoning his "life energy." That would take him one dimension higher. He refined this energy, transforming it into what people called "fighting spirit"—that would raise his attack one dimension further.

An aura was already leaking out from within his body, forming a glow around him.

"Huh?"

Earnest blinked in surprise. She'd asked him to prove himself, sure. But what was this guy trying to do? It was almost like…

*"Haaaaaaah…"*

More energy continued to gather around Blade's body. Now it wasn't just Earnest. The entire senior class was starting to tremble with fear. Only Sophie looked cool and unaffected as usual.

*"Haaaaaaah..."*

Blade's spirit seemed to rise up without end. The sheer pressure of his energy made pebbles on the ground around him float into the air, defying gravity. Lightning crackled around him, arcing between the small stones.

"Whoa! Whoa?! Whoaaaa?!" Earnest panicked.

This move... She had never seen it before, but she had heard of it. This must be a skill of the "dragon-destroying" type—one meant for combating those gigantic beasts—said to be the greatest skill a person could muster on their own.

Her face twisted in fear. Sophie, next to her, showed no expression. But she wasn't uninterested—she was watching, quietly astonished in her own way.

"Wha— Stop!" Earnest flung herself forward to put an end to this. But she was too late.

*"Haaaah!!"*

Blade brought his sword down.

This was Dragon Eater, the second of his dragon-destroying skills. A superpowered spiral of fighting spirit whirled and roared as it shot out ahead of him, extending as far as the eye could see. It was a double whirlpool of lethal force, strong enough to pierce even the tough skin of a mighty dragon.

The magic-metal armor caught in this twin whirl instantly disintegrated. The technique, designed to consume even a dragon, smashed against the Proving Ground's outer wall. There it was stopped by several layers of defensive barriers, but only for a moment, before it sliced through them like they were made of paper. The stone wall of another building was crushed—and still the whirling beam shot forward.

Eventually, the plumes of smoke began to clear, and the pebbles and bits of earth fell back to the ground. Earnest finally dared to open her eyes after shutting them during the attack.

"Ah!"

That was when the wind blast from Dragon Eater hit her. Parts of her outfit were torn off—she rushed to cover up her body.

The other students had crouched and taken refuge as well. Only Sophie was still standing, looking on in her unaffected way; but the whirling dust was starting to get all over her face.

Blade's blast had gouged through the ground in a straight line nearly a hundred feet long. Beyond the circular hole in the wall, they could see the next school building over—and another circular hole in *that* wall, revealing the bottom half of an upstairs classroom and the top half of a downstairs one. They were both unoccupied, thankfully...but the fountain in the courtyard below had been torn apart and was now spraying water haphazardly into the air.

Earnest looked up and turned, aghast, to Blade.

"Hmm... Not my best," he said.

Blade hefted up his sword, tapping it against his shoulder. On the third tap, it crumbled apart. The metal collapsed into its component molecules, disintegrating into ash from the raised tip down.

"Oh... Looks like it couldn't take it."

He'd just unleashed a marvelous skill, and his only comment was about his sword's durability. And when he'd said "not my best" a moment ago, was he talking about the force of that strike...? He probably was, wasn't he? Just how much further could he take it...?

Blade, however, was stunned by his lackluster attempt. Normally, he could do a lot more damage, but...ah, well. He was still recovering, he told himself.

He turned to face the crowd and just happened to make eye contact with Earnest as she looked up.

"Ah..."

Blade had finally noticed. Starting with Earnest, he looked at each of the other students in turn. All of their expressions said the exact same thing. Once he had checked all twelve or so of their faces, Blade broke into a cold sweat.

*Oh crap, oh crap, I... Oh crap...*

Apparently, he had overdone it once again.

"Ah, um... I'm normal, okay? I'm just an average, normal person."

He *really* wanted them all to see him as normal. But he was a little too late for that.

## ○ Scene VIII: In the Dining Hall

It had been several days since Blade joined this school, and a few things had happened in the meantime. He had made some friends; he had been promoted from the junior to the senior class; and he had made some mistakes (or rather, committed large-scale property damage) in both of them... But despite these errors and trip-ups, he was starting to get used to his new life.

Right now, for example, he was in the dining hall for lunch, looking around the crowded chamber for a free seat. At the moment, by far the most important thing on his mind was where he was going to sit. It was such an incredibly *normal* thing for a student to be concerned about. So blatantly average.

There was a mountain of food on his tray, perhaps enough for three people. The dining hall at the student dorms allowed you to take and eat as much as you pleased, so his tray was piled high with meat, meat, and more meat. There was also a little plate of veggies on the side, which he'd added after the lunch lady yelled at him. The main dish that day was some kind of unfamiliar brown sauce ladled over rice. It was called "curry," apparently, and had only recently been brought over from the southern lands. With the Overlord gone and peace returning, trade had begun to flourish once again. All kinds of new things were flowing in.

Unfortunately, this was the peak lunch rush, and it was proving difficult to find a seat—but then Blade's eyes stopped on a faraway table. Shockingly, every chair at it was free.

"Oh, look at that! This whole table is open!"

He planted himself down in a chair, and only then did he realize there was a single girl sitting diagonally across from him. A girl with a striking red silhouette. A girl who was already glaring at him with untold force. Blade had once accidentally fallen into a red dragon's nest, and the Great

Dragon's eyes—filled with rage at having its sleep interrupted—had felt just like this.

"Yo," he said, raising up a fork. This earned him an even more menacing look.

Earnest, after shooting him a glare that might have killed someone weaker, silently went back to her meal, her fork listlessly traveling between her plate and her lips. Blade copied her, doing much the same thing with his spoon, passively noting how she always seemed to be glaring at him whenever they met. He had no idea what he'd done to deserve such treatment. He thought about it a moment, bringing a hand to his chest...but no great ideas occurred to him.

This large, broad table was big enough to seat ten people, and he was sitting here with nobody but her. The entire dining hall was packed, and yet the two of them seemed strangely isolated.

"Oh, heyyy!"

A little ways away, Blade spotted some familiar faces—Claire, Yessica, Clayde, and Kassim. They were in different classes now, but this was the quartet he had first become friends with. They were all standing, trays in hand; he waved at them, signaling that there was open space where he was. But they shook their heads, refusing to take another step. What were they trying to tell him? He had no idea. He thought shaking your head meant *no*, but that had to be wrong, didn't it?

"Everybody's afraid of me," Earnest grumbled abruptly.

"Huh? Afraid? Of you?"

She was finally talking to him. Blade's eyes sparkled. He moved one seat over, positioning himself right in front of her.

"This table's kind of exclusively for me."

"Why is that?"

"Let me make one thing clear... I didn't ask for this."

"So why?"

It was news to him that Earnest was feared. Why would that be? There was nothing scary about her. She might have a habit of shooting people mean looks...as mean as a hungry Great Dragon, in fact...but still.

"Wait, are you maybe...like, being bullied or something?"

"Who? Me?" Earnest smiled. There was a darkness to her expression, however, which only deepened Blade's concern.

"Well, if you ever feel like someone's bullying you...tell me, all right? 'Cause I'll go talk to them."

"You...you're a real idiot, aren't you?"

She looked up from her lunch and glared at him. *She called me an idiot? Huh? I was seriously worrying about her. Guess I was wrong.*

Claire's group came a little closer, but they never did join Blade and Earnest, instead sitting down at an adjacent table that happened to clear out. He tried motioning for them to join, but they just shook their heads vigorously. *That* really *looks like the sign for* no. *But it can't be—so what is it?*

"...I take it back."

"Huh?" said Blade. "What was that?"

Blade had to ask for clarification. He was too busy repeating the cycle of "come here," *shake, shake, shake*; "come here," *shake, shake, shake* with Claire and the gang to fully understand Earnest's quiet words.

"I *said*...!" Earnest raised her voice for a moment, but quickly stopped, then started over from the beginning. "I *said*...that I take it back."

"Take what back?"

"Look, I *mean*...!" Earnest blushed. Maybe she realized she was getting nowhere repeating herself. She stopped and tried again.

"I mean...like saying how you cheated...the admission system...and stuff!" She was holding back, but she still couldn't keep from turning up the volume.

"...You said that?" Blade raised an eyebrow. He had no memory of it.

"*Yes!*"

She was no longer holding back. She slapped the table hard with one hand.

"Look, what is your problem anyway? Huh? I've been totally preoccupied thinking about that this whole time! And you're saying you don't even remember?!"

Her glare bored into him, deeper than ever. This was beyond "hungry Great Dragon" levels. The demonic glint in her eyes was akin to that of an

Ancient Dragon. Even Blade was finally forced to conclude that Earnest was angry.

"Hey…what are you so mad about?"

"*What*, you ask?"

She glared at him again. That wasn't such a big deal, but it was starting to unnerve Blade. She had just reached down for her sword—in fact, she was grasping the handle.

Unlike the other students, she carried her sword even into the dining hall. Having one's weapon close by at all times was a given for anyone who lived and died on the battlefield, but she was the only one in the whole school acting on this "given." Blade, of course, was just another regular, average student, so he never carried a sword outside of training.

*You see? I'm normal. A regular person. Blindingly average…*

"Wait, wait, wait! Don't draw that thing in here! What…what're you even gonna *do* with that sword?! You gonna strike me down right here?!"

"I already tried to once!"

"Huuuh?! When?!"

"You *dodged* it!"

"Huuuh?! No way! When?!"

It had happened right after he patted her on the head. Earnest had come at him with a lethal strike. He had unconsciously darted to the side to avoid it, not even registering it in his memory. You can't keep thinking about every move you make in battle if you want to cut it as a Hero. Not that he was one now or anything.

Some snickering could be heard from the seats around them. Earnest glared fiercely in the direction of the sound, and it promptly stopped. Now aware of the attention, she calmed down and took her hand off her sword.

"I really don't remember…"

At that comment from Blade, however, Earnest's hand slipped right back to the handle.

"Whoa, whoa, hold it! I do, I do, I *do* remember! I do! I swear that I—I—I *do*! I *swear*!" He really didn't remember, but he thought it prudent to lie.

"See?" Earnest looked at Blade. She didn't look angry or upset.

*Oh,* thought Blade, *she's capable of smiling?* This was a fresh surprise.

"You…have a decent amount of ability, I will admit," said Earnest. "It's unconventional, yes, but I can't deny it… I wouldn't have slashed at you otherwise. Not unless I knew you could avoid it… See?"

She stabbed at her pasta as she spoke, cruelly spinning it around her fork like it was her archnemesis.

*Oh. I guess it's okay to eat again.*

Following her lead, Blade began to eat again. This curry sauce poured over rice, and this sliced filet of fried chicken—"katsu," they called it—placed on top… This dish…was *so* good. *So* good. Curry was *delicious*. Even better with a piece of katsu. Katsu curry was like *ambrosia*. Whoever invented it was a genius.

But as Blade lost himself in his choice of lunch—

"And certainly…you have enough skill…to be at the bottom rank…of the senior class…"

—Earnest started muttering again. Her voice was too soft for Blade to make out much, and he wasn't listening anyway. The katsu curry was just too good.

"I'm sorry… I take it back. Not the bottom rank. You'd probably place a little above average… Or perhaps, near the bottom of the top… I mean, ummm…"

She just kept stabbing and spinning her pasta around, not bothering to eat any, as she continued to mutter away.

"…No, but…!" Her head shot up, her voice suddenly gaining volume. "But I just want to say that you have the skills to be in the top group—"

Blade lifted his head up from the curry plate just long enough to ask, "Sorry, did you say something?"

"*Why, youuuuu!!*"

Earnest slammed her hands on the table. The plates lifted into the air for just a moment.

*Whoa. Neat.*

All sound in the dining hall suddenly stopped cold. The entire room fell into a profound hush.

*What does this mean?*

Blade swiveled his head to look around the chamber. His eyes settled upon Claire's group at the table next to his—they were all pale and quivering. No more weird shakes of the head, either. The cacophony of the crowded dining hall had suddenly been overtaken by sheer silence, and Blade had no idea why.

"…Ahem."

Earnest very deliberately cleared her throat, as if this sudden shift in atmosphere was her fault or something. *But that can't be right*, Blade thought. *Maybe she's just overly self-conscious?* He didn't dare say as much, however. He knew it'd only earn him another vicious glare.

After a few moments, the hall began to regain its clamor.

"I can't *believe* this!" Earnest said, plopping back into her seat.

Blade observed their plates carefully, hoping they'd be thrown up again, but no such luck. He was a little disappointed. It seemed her rear end didn't have enough weight to it.

Grabbing her fork, Earnest indignantly began to eat—not just spinning her pasta endlessly like before, but actually eating it. Her food gradually began to disappear.

Blade had already just about finished, so he rested his chin atop his folded hands and watched her. She was eating fast, like all good soldiers do. Eat when you can, then rest when you can—words to live by for anyone in an army. You never knew when you might be called on to engage in constant battle for an unknown amount of time.

…As he thought this, it dawned on him that he was still mentally in "battle" mode. But he wasn't a soldier, right? He was just a regular person. He'd heard that this school was meant to bring up champions, though. That meant she, too, was likely a champion in training…

As he watched Earnest tear into her meal, taking out all her anger on the food, Blade had a thought. There was something he wanted to tell her, and now seemed like a good opportunity.

"You know, I'm really grateful."

"Huh?" Earnest put her fork down and blinked at him.

"For you being here. You've been a big help."

"Huh? What?"

Her eyes, usually squinting with resentment, were now perfect circles. "Wh-why...why are you telling me *this* all of a sudden?"

"I mean... I'm a midsemester transfer student, right?"

That's what she'd told him—and right when he was trying his best to be normal and inconspicuous. But he was actually standing out like a sore thumb, as Earnest was quick to point out. Her advice had been very helpful, something he still appreciated now.

"Midsemester or not, we don't really get transfer students here—"

"I thought that we could be friends."

"Huh? Friends? With who? Huh? What? W-w-with me...?" Earnest's mouth was open as wide as her eyes.

"Yeah. And now we're eating together. That means we're pals, right?"

Blade raised his spoon up as he spoke, using it to point at himself and Earnest in succession. Then he began finishing up his lunch. The katsu curry was all gone, but the salad the lunch lady had insisted on giving him was still there. He packed that away, too.

"F...f-f-friends?"

Earnest looked like something unbelievable had just happened. She turned away and stared at a random point in space. The other students in the dining hall all looked down, not wanting to wind up in her line of sight.

As far as Blade was concerned, facing each other across the same table and eating together meant you were friends. But why wouldn't Claire and the others join them? They were his friends, too, and there was all this extra space. He turned toward them again...only for their rapidly shaking heads to make a return appearance.

That was when Earnest finally snapped out of it. "W-well...I guess we could...maybe...be friends, but..."

*So easy.*

*The Empress went down in no time flat.*

*He barely had to try.*

Voiceless thoughts erupted in the minds of those sitting around them... but Blade and Earnest were none the wiser.

## ○ Scene IX: Earnest's Room

Earnest entered her room and shut the door, cutting herself off from the hallway. Now that she was alone, she finally let out the sigh she had been saving up all this time. She could feel herself loosening up a bit.

After removing her sword belt, she placed her beloved blade against the wall. Then she took out her hair clip, freeing her long red hair as she undid her top just a little to release her pushed-in chest.

"Whew..."

She finally felt like herself again.

Student lodging, as a rule, involved two to four people staying in large rooms, but Earnest was allowed a personal chamber as a special case. It wasn't anything she specifically requested—it was just that nobody wanted to be roommates with the famed Empress, and this was the natural result.

She was grateful for it, though. Around other people, she had to fulfill her role as the Empress. If someone lived with her, she'd need to keep up the act even in her own room. It was her destiny to remain at the top. The Flamings belonged to one of the most prestigious noble families in the land. Their lineage of knights had long served the king, both secretly and openly, and was now one of the kingdom's greatest military clans. And Earnest Flaming was slated to be the next head of the family.

Because of her position, it was expected that she would stand at the top in all things. It was her duty. She needed to be a model for the entire student body, taking the lead and demonstrating what it meant to be an exemplary student and—

"Whew..."

She reached out for the pitcher that sat atop the sideboard. Not bothering with a cup, she brought it directly to her lips and began chugging. There was no way she could *ever* do something like this around others.

Earnest always maintained a policy of strict self-discipline. Being at the top was, to be honest, nothing more than a result—the result of controlling herself more powerfully than anyone else. That had led to all her achievements—it had been almost automatic. As a noble from a clan of knights, she had certain duties, of course. But Earnest had an even greater calling, one that demanded an even higher standard of discipline.

That was why she never made friends. And she was content with that.

"But *him*..."

That new transfer student, of all people... He had called her his *friend*. They'd only shared one meal. How idiotic.

As Empress, she couldn't recall a single time when she had shared a table with other students her age. It wasn't that she was purposely keeping her distance—the other students did that for her. But here *he* was, stomping right up to her, taking a seat, and calling her his friend like it was his right to decide.

She had seen for herself what he'd done on the Proving Ground. Only ten or so others had witnessed it with her; it was being called a "mystery explosion" by the rest of the student body. He had broken through the Proving Ground's multilayered magic barrier and half destroyed an entire school building—all by himself. If that became public knowledge, the whole school would be in an uproar.

Only a champion could do something like that, and no student was supposed to be at that level. But Earnest wasn't kidding herself anymore. She knew that hadn't been some kind of freak accident. She had to acknowledge his abilities. He might very well be second only to her in this school.

And he had called her his friend. Maybe she could allow it. If he claimed to be Earnest Flaming's friend, he'd *better* be capable of blowing a giant hole in a school building. Otherwise, he'd just be making her look bad. The damage to her reputation would be incalculable.

And that meant...she had done it. She had made a friend. For the first time. A friend. *A friend.* That's what he had called her—a friend.

"A friend… But then… Oh, what should I do?" she muttered to herself.

She had just brought her hands up to her chest, lost in her emotions, when suddenly—

*Clatter, clatter…*

—there was a noise in her room. Nobody else was inside. The clattering sound had come from her sword, propped against the wall.

This was the magic sword Asmodeus, imbued with flame magic; an heirloom passed down through generations of Flamings. Earnest had become its "possessor," and that was a big reason why she had been named the next family head at such a young age. Whoever possessed Asmodeus always led the Flaming clan in the service of the king. That was the rule.

The vibrations of the sword were a reminder—Earnest was loosening her heart too much. The realization made her shudder. She promptly reined in her emotions, biting her lip and chasing away the feelings floating around in her mind.

"I need to remain at the top…like all those of the Flaming clan…"

She whispered this over and over in the darkened room, as if chanting a curse—with herself as the target.

## ○ Scene X: Practical Study Time

It was time for another practical study session.

Blade liked these sessions a lot more than he did the lectures. He enjoyed just being able to move around. He had lain motionless in bed for several months at the hospital after his fight against the Overlord, so his body had atrophied in all kinds of ways. It'd likely take several more months to get back in shape.

*But then, do I really need to worry about that? I'm a normal person now. It's not like I gotta duke it out with another Overlord. He was* really *strong. It's a miracle I'm even alive. Though I'm sure he's thinking the same thing right about now.*

"Yo!"

Blade raised a hand in greeting at the red figure as soon as she entered his sight. He had just made friends with Earnest the day before. At least he thought they were friends... Huh? Weird, she was ignoring him.

"Yo! Yo! Yo!"

He circled her, hopping around to get her attention. She must not have seen him or something.

*Glare.*

She shot him a blood-curdling look. This time, her eyes emitted a force so strong it manifested physically. He could feel his hair blowing backward. For just a moment, he had a new slicked-back hairstyle. He had once met an old crone who could fire off top-level flame magic just by staring at something, and he was sure Earnest could pull that off, too, if she kept at it.

"What could you *possibly* be doing?" she asked, frowning as hard as she could.

"Just saying hello... Yo!"

His arm flew up.

"I told you yesterday that I recognized your skills, didn't I?"

"Y-yeah...?"

Blade wasn't sure he remembered that. But he could easily imagine her glare boring holes in him again if he admitted it, so he kept quiet. *Ain't I smart?* he thought.

"You'll be joining this group," she said, gesturing to several students gathered around her.

The group in question gave off a particularly strong presence even amid the senior class. He remembered the girl wearing the cape exactly as blue as her hair. He'd become friends with her a little while ago; he remembered her name and everything.

"Oh, it's you, Sophie!" he shouted without thinking.

She met his line with a confused quirk of her eyebrow.

"I—I am Blade!" he continued.

"I know," she replied bluntly. Such a cold response would put a damper on anyone else, but not Blade. He was delighted. She remembered his name! That made her a real friend!

"What are you doing?! Line up! You're wasting everybody's valuable time!"

Earnest dressed them both down. Even Blade could tell she was angry.

"Did I upset her somehow?" he asked Sophie, shrugging his shoulders.

"I don't know," she replied curtly, not even bothering to shrug.

## ○ Scene XI: Senior Class

They were forced to wait in line for quite a while.

It wasn't like in the junior class, of course, where everyone stood in a crisp, square formation with military precision; they were simply standing around in a group. Earnest even had a hand on her hip as she scowled at the others.

Blade got the feeling his classmates here didn't think very much of their instructors. You could find such people in the army, or anywhere else—exceptional talents who chafed at rules they saw as beneath them. Blade had teamed up with "irregular forces" like that—people with more than their fair share of quirks—for most of his career, and he was pretty used to them by now.

Class was taking a long time to begin. They must have been waiting for someone really important.

Earnest's stare bored into the training instructor. He seemed to physically wither, his eyes darting around before finally focusing in one direction.

"Y...Your Majesty!"

Everyone's heads turned at once. There he was, calmly walking toward them, a beautiful female attendant to either side. It was the chancellor of this academy...or, more broadly speaking, their nation's king. And thanks to this nation—or rather, its king—bringing an end to the great war started by the Overlord, he could very well become the leader of the entire continent in time.

Earnest stood at attention, her heels briskly clacking against the floor. *Oh, so she'll do that for the king, at least.* Blade was a little impressed. Come to think of it, hadn't she glared at him on his first day, after he caused her to lose her chance to speak with the king? Did she really want to talk to a bum like him that badly? He was all bluff and bluster, flying from one wild idea to the next and expecting other people to clean up his mess.

"It is a great honor," exclaimed Earnest, speaking on behalf of the other students, "for you to sit in on our class, Chancellor!"

"Ha-ha-ha! Well, it's my job. I *am* the chancellor."

The king looked at Blade. Blade responded by hiding behind Earnest, ensuring the king had to look at her instead.

"But...yes, you seem to be working hard. It gladdens me to see it."

"Yes, my liege! I am devoting everything to my studies, in order to lay the groundwork for the next generation of our kingdom!"

Earnest was giving as sincere a reply as she could. Blade was busy trying to keep himself hidden and ensure the king's eyes were focused squarely on her. His Majesty, of course, meant his comment for Blade—and, sadly, Blade wasn't putting in anything like his best effort. He had no intention of using the school for "rehabilitation," as the king had put it. But when it came to making friends and being a normal person, he was doing everything he could—*everything*.

"I humbly suggest," said Earnest, "that we flesh out our team of instructors, Your Majesty. If we want to extract everything we possibly can from our student body, there is only so much we can achieve with our current faculty."

*She said it! She really said it! She's polite to the king and all, but she doesn't care one bit about the teachers.*

The way the instructor cowered at this only made him look more pathetic. Maybe Earnest had a point. The instructor didn't seem very reliable to Blade. He looked like the type who wouldn't last a day on the front lines.

"Mmm, yes, I will certainly look into the instructor issue. Today, however, I'd like to see a demonstration of your abilities. I haven't been chancellor for long, after all. I don't know how good your kung fu is yet."

"Our...kung fu, my liege?" asked Earnest.

"Indeed. I mean the results of your training, of course."

"Ah. Well, in that case..." Earnest looked around the senior class, thinking for a few moments before making a suggestion. "What do you think about us holding a tournament? ...Under real battle conditions, of course."

"Mmm, that sounds delightful! A truly excellent idea!"

"I am honored to hear that," she replied, curtsying politely like the refined noble girl she was. The gesture surprised Blade. "I was hoping to see the abilities of our new transfer student as well," she continued.

Her face was pointed right at the king as she spoke, but she probably meant her words for Blade, given that she kept him firmly in the corner of her vision.

*Ughhh...* Blade groaned inwardly. *This* again? Didn't he just test his strength around her a little while ago? He'd already shown off his "kung fu" or whatever. Since the advanced class was supposedly three dimensions above the junior class, he'd turned his attack up three notches. It seemed like Dragon Eater had been a little too much, but it was only the second weakest in the family of dragon-destroying skills, so it shouldn't have been that bad.

*I just don't know how to go easy, all right?!*

And now they were talking about a tournament? What even was that—a competition? Having grown up on the battlefield, Blade didn't know much about social niceties. Heroes spent more of their time in wild wastelands and dank dungeons than in town. The events held in cities were dazzling and brilliant to him, something only ever glimpsed in passing as a Hero.

His lack of enthusiasm must have been obvious, because the king's eyes began to glint.

"Right!" he said. "How about I offer a reward to help motivate everyone, then?"

"A...reward?" asked Earnest. "If I may, Majesty, we in the senior class do not train for our own personal gain—"

"And I've got a good one in mind, too. The winner of this tournament will receive personal training from the Hero!"

*Ughhh...* Blade groaned inwardly once again.

"Huh? Hero...? You mean *that* Hero...? The vanquisher of the Overlord...?"

"And what other Hero would I be referring to, hmm? *He* is the only Hero I know. And he happens to be a personal friend of mine, too. If I ask him for a favor, he'll come running!"

*No I won't.*

"H-he will...? The Hero himself? He'd train me?" Earnest's eyes shot open. She looked like she could hardly believe what she was hearing.

"Indeed," he said, nodding. "On my name as king, I promise you."

*There he goes again, that bastard. And he's got that "leave everything to me" smile he used to trick everyone—allied and hostile nations alike.*

*Don't make promises on my behalf, old man...*

In a way, this *did* motivate him a little. If someone else won the tournament, he'd have a lot of explaining to do. Everyone would find out he was the former Hero, and *then* what would happen? ...Well, maybe nothing so bad. It wouldn't be the end of the world...but it wouldn't exactly fill him with glee, either. It'd put a serious damper on his serene life as a regular student—a *serious* damper. And for that matter, he wasn't even a Hero anymore. He was just a normal person, an average citizen—a student.

*Right. Let's win this.*

Blade's mind was made up. He didn't know much about the senior class's abilities, though. And he'd need to win while keeping his moves as gentle, as easy, as *normal* as possible, so that he wouldn't be too conspicuous. It sounded really difficult to pull off, but he had no other choice.

## ○ Scene XII: Tournament

Someone drew out a tournament bracket in the sandy ground. Blade expected them to draw straws to decide the matchups, but instead Earnest wrote in all the names, choosing the pairings herself. None of the students seemed bothered by this, and the instructor—currently trying to make himself invisible in a far corner of the Proving Ground—didn't voice any complaints, either.

It turned out that Earnest was largely responsible for determining the senior class's curriculum. She, as Empress and leader of the school, had the exclusive right to decide what kind of training they did, and for how long. As a result, she was the natural choice to determine the tournament's matchups as well. Presumably, she had paired people up in order to create the most impressive battles possible for the king. Though Blade, who had no idea what any of his classmates could do, couldn't be sure.

Soon, it was time for the first battle.

Two students faced off in the center of the vast Proving Ground, surrounded by their watching classmates (Blade included). Knowing that Earnest was prone to unpredictable fits of rage, Blade had feared she'd come slashing away at him from the very first fight...but they weren't even in the same block of the bracket. If they fought at all, it would be in the final match. Since Earnest had decided all the matchups, Blade felt there must be some reason she'd laid it out that way.

Blade didn't fight in the first battle, but Earnest did. She took on a dashing young man carrying a worryingly huge lance. He was the sort of man who didn't bother putting his arms through the sleeves of his coat, preferring to drape it over his shoulders so it'd flutter heroically in the wind. Between this affected attitude and his mild-mannered looks, he didn't seem like he'd be all that strong in a fight—but once the match began, Blade could tell right away that he was decently talented.

The lancer could handle his chosen weapon with astonishing skill. It was large and heavy and had hidden compartments containing secret extras. Blade was sure it was a one-of-a-kind piece—not standard issue. Earnest, meanwhile, was carrying a sword with an unusual wavelike shape, the same one she always kept close to her hip. A sort of dark haze seemed to emanate from its blade, suggesting some sort of magical force. When it was unsheathed, one could feel its ominous aura like small pinpricks on the skin.

After a couple of opening clashes, the two fighters separated, sizing each other up.

"I want to see a real effort from you, Leonard," the Empress said, her sword at the ready.

"Oh brother. I don't really want to point this lance at a woman, you know. But if I don't try my best, you're only going to be angrier with me, so..."

The dashing man called Leonard activated something in his weapon, pulling hard at a handle with a cord attached to it. With a roar, the spear's tip began to revolve at high speed.

"Whoa!" Blade said, pointing at it. "Cool!" He turned to the rest of the audience, as if to say "Get a load of that thing!" But they all either ignored him, stayed silent, or shushed him.

*How could anyone not be excited by that? It's a drill spear!*

*...Oh, right. They've already seen it before, haven't they? I just got here, so I didn't know.*

Only the king seemed to share his opinion, and he shot Blade a self-satisfied nod. Blade, not wanting the king to acknowledge him at all, if possible, decided to keep quiet.

But the drill lance wasn't the weapon's only flashy gimmick. There were openings along its length that looked a bit like exhaust nozzles. *Could it be...?* Blade kept watching, anticipation building in his mind.

"Ladies and gentlemen! Let the show begin!"

With those scripted introductory remarks, the dashing Leonard prepared to launch a strike. Earnest responded with a bold smile. The distance between them was perfect for a spear attack. With a sword, you could only reach a few yards, and that was *with* an opening step or two—but that and a little beyond was the range spears were *born* to fight in.

When it came to fights, the first side to act usually had the advantage. Earnest was fighting at ideal spear range, and even worse, she seemed willing to let Leonard have the first strike. What sort of strategy could she have in mind? Blade watched curiously.

Leonard the lancer advanced in a straight line. The nozzles of his weapon spat out searing fire, accelerating the spear forward. Just then—

"*Haaah!*"

—Earnest swung her sword at what appeared to be nothing at all, well out of range of Leonard. But then a wave of red energy shot out from her blade, forming a blazing-hot ball of fire that engulfed the lancer as he advanced.

*Whoa, whoa, whoa, whoa! She killed him!*

Blade genuinely believed Leonard was dead. That's how intense the fireball was. Earnest had said the tournament would simulate actual battle... *But, wow, they're really fighting to the death here?* "Actual" was right. Blade was impressed.

After putting his hands together and saying a quick prayer for the lancer, Blade thought over what he had just seen. Earnest's sword was of particular interest. He'd thought it was more than a regular blade, that it had magic...but it was *so* powerful. With a weapon like that, you wouldn't even need a magic caster in your party. The only people he had seen carrying magic swords *that* powerful were the generals in the Overlord's army.

*I see. She's talented with a sword, and her weapon packs the firepower of a high wizard's barrage, and with no casting time required. No wonder the Empress rules over the whole student body.*

"Boy, Earnest, you didn't need to go that far... I thought I was going to die for a moment there."

*Oh, he's alive?*

The smoke cleared after a few moments, revealing the lancer, covered in soot but very much still living. After speaking, however, Leonard collapsed in a heap.

"Laaame."

"All bark and no bite, huh?"

"Oh, Leonard's always like that."

The audience's reaction was harsh. Nobody seemed too concerned about him. A group of medics came up and carted him off on a stretcher, but

Blade doubted he was hurt all that badly. He wasn't sure how the boy had managed to weather such intense flame, but Blade had to hand it to him. The senior class was something else. Maybe he had some kind of unique skill or ability that helped him survive—and Earnest, knowing that, had turned the intensity all the way up.

Blade was relieved. Nobody was dying here. This was *simulated* actual battle, not *actual* battle. If they were doing *actual* battle in class, it'd only be repeating the past for him. It wouldn't be any different from his days as a Hero. He fought a lot back then, and it was all the real deal, so naturally he'd had to kill a lot, too. Not because he wanted to, of course.

*...This is much better. Everyone here is normal. School is the best.*

The battles continued one after another. One would end, and another would start right away. Blade fought a few of his own, against both boys and girls. Since this was simulated battle, he selected a one-handed sword with a dull blade and went as easy as he reasonably could. With the girls in particular, he made sure to win by striking the back of their necks—and even then, he took great pains to ensure it didn't leave a bruise.

Sixteen people participated in the first round, fighting eight duels. This decreased to eight people and four duels in the second round, and then four and two in the third. Everyone was using their choice of specialized weapon or skill—mostly swords, but some had lances, maces, or war hammers. There was even an archer. Getting to see so many disparate battle styles in one place fascinated Blade.

One of the other students in the audience explained to him that the second-to-last round was called the "semifinal," while the last one was the "final." Blade had just wrapped up his semifinal match, and now he was watching the other one.

There, in the center of the Proving Ground, red was facing off against blue. The red figure, of course, was Earnest, and Blade knew the name of the blue figure, too. It was Sophie, and up until now, she had always been fighting at the same time as Blade. This was his first chance to really see her in action.

Right away, her battle style surprised him. She was barehanded. Blade had seen all kinds of weapons so far—swords, spears, maces, arrows, a drill lance—the whole gamut. Earnest had likely considered that when she drew up the brackets. Each pairing was well matched, with no one weapon enjoying a huge advantage over the opponent's.

But now, in Earnest's semifinal, she was fighting someone with no weapon at all. *She can't be serious...* Sophie wasn't completely unarmed, however; she appeared to have wrist gauntlets of some kind on her hands. But her offensive range ended at her fingertips and went no farther.

Seeing Sophie face off barehanded against Earnest and her sword was a shock to Blade. Earnest had fought a lancer with her sword earlier, but she was so much more powerful than Leonard, she had easily made up for the disadvantage. Did Sophie have the kind of skill that would allow her to do the same...?

Blade left the ring of onlookers, moving closer to the two fighters to gain a better view. He was within about a referee's range of the action, but there was no referee overseeing this fight; the fighters were obliged to call out their own wins and losses.

Now closer, Blade could overhear the participants conversing with each other.

"No cheating, all right?" Earnest said for some reason.

"Aren't *you* the one cheating with that?" countered Sophie.

Judging by where her indifferent gaze was pointed, she must have been referring to the magic sword in Earnest's hand. At first, Blade wasn't sure what she meant, but after thinking it over, something dawned on him. From his experience as a Hero, he tended to calculate an opponent's strength as the sum of their core abilities plus those of their weapon. He had never been in a position to sit back and conjecture how strong someone would be on their own. When the Hero invaded an enemy stronghold, its defenders weren't likely to leave their gear behind when they confronted him.

*Ahhh, the Overlord's scepter sure packed a mean punch...*

That said, carrying a super-powerful weapon came at a commensurate price. It might greatly fatigue its user, or it might place a ghastly curse upon them. Maybe the sword had to accept its user as its "chosen possessor" first.

But Earnest didn't seem to have any such issues. So what was Sophie talking about? What was the meaning behind their terse conversation?

Earnest stared back at Sophie, her gaze intense. This wasn't just her standard hole-boring glare; this one could have blasted out a whole quarry. Did Sophie's accusation that she'd brought a "cheat" weapon to the fight rankle her that much? Either way, it looked like Sophie had won the psychological battle before the fight even began.

"Don't worry," Sophie said. "I won't use it."

What was the "cheat"? What wasn't Sophie using? Blade was lost, his questions unanswered as the battle got underway.

The first to strike was Earnest, still burning with rage. She swung mightily, as if trying to slice her opponent lengthwise in two, over and over again. Sophie leaped and twisted to dodge the blows, and when that wasn't enough, she deflected Earnest's blade with her gauntlets, altering its path just enough to avoid damage.

At first, Earnest was only slashing and Sophie only dodging. A streak of blue darted around the arena, chased after by a streak of red—and with every zigzag movement came the clanging of metal, lagging a little behind. The blue streak, composed of Sophie's cape and scarf, fluttered out behind her—but every swing from Earnest's sword seemed to shorten it a bit, cutting it to ribbons.

Sophie was forced to focus entirely on self-defense, but only her clothing was being struck; the air was filled not with blood but bits of fabric. That was a good thing. This was just a tournament after all; they were still in class.

And so, despite challenging a sword-wielder barehanded, Sophie was putting up a pretty good fight.

Blade's instincts told him that if an unarmed fighter wanted to beat someone with a sword, they'd need to be around three times as skilled. The two here were a decent match in ability, but they weren't exactly equal, either. For one thing, Sophie had failed to mount any offense so far.

Blade had thought at first that Sophie might have some winning strategy in mind, or enough superior skill to best Earnest barehanded, but that wasn't the case. The power gap between the blade and her fists was slowly putting her on the ropes. If she made the wrong move, she could lose a forearm, so Blade understood why she wasn't punching like mad out there— Wait, this was still class, right? Surely, dismemberment was off the table.

Blade was confused. *I don't get it. How far are you allowed to go in class, exactly? Earnest is using a real, lethal sword that could easily lop off a limb or two if she stopped paying attention...*

Now Earnest had seized all the initiative. Blade had been expecting Sophie to pull out some kind of cheat move as Earnest had implied, but it seemed that wasn't happening. Earnest was simply making ample use of her magic sword's capabilities, launching fireballs whenever Sophie attempted to back away from her. Dodging those required Sophie to take major evasive maneuvers, leaving her more open and pushing her ever closer to the brink.

*Maybe a few more seconds, tops,* Blade thought.

Sophie held out for a good half minute longer. But the battle ended with a sudden coda. Sophie fell backward, and Earnest placed the tip of her sword against her opponent's throat.

"...I give," said Sophie, looking as unaffected as ever as she sat sprawled out on the ground.

"Very good." Earnest sighed deeply. Her breathing was ragged, the sweat visible on her forehead.

Sophie stood up and patted the dust off her body. She reeled in her scarf, then looked at the far end of it, all cut up into pieces. She examined her chopped-up cape, which now looked something like a bead curtain. Her breathing was perfectly normal. She never wasted a movement; every evasive maneuver was achieved with the minimum amount of work. The battle would've ended long ago otherwise.

Looking at it from that perspective, it was no longer so clear who had actually won.

"Right! Now it's your turn!"

Earnest's sword swished through the air, its tip pointed at Blade.

"Huh? Why? ...Oh, right."

Now he remembered. The semifinal was called that because it was the match before the final. Earnest had just won her semifinal, so now it was his turn to fight her in this "final" or whatever.

"You may…have that huge finisher…," she said between ragged gulps of breath, "but it won't hurt me if it…can't touch me!"

She must have been talking about Dragon Eater. And, yes, it *did* take some time to properly charge up—longer than a typical enemy would stand politely by and wait. It wasn't the kind of thing he could use in battle unless he had allies nearby backing him up. But Blade didn't really consider it a "finisher." It was just a little trick, really—the second weakest of the dragon-destroying skills.

The king, who had been bored and distracted, chatting with one of his ministers, noticed that Blade was up. He promptly turned his attention to the fight and moved back to his seat. He opened his eyes wide and gazed intensely at the combatants.

*Well, great.*

"We don't really have to do this, do we?" said Blade.

"Oh, we *do*!" Earnest said, pointing at him with her sword.

It sounded like she already wanted him dead. Pinching the tip of her sword with two fingers, he moved the blade off to the side. She really shouldn't be doing that, he thought, unless she really *did* mean to slice him up.

"But—see? We're out of time."

Blade swung his sword toward the clock in one corner of the Proving Ground. It was well past the end of class; they were already fifteen minutes into lunch break. Conducting fourteen duels had a way of eating up time, after all.

*I'm famished. I gotta get something to eat… Isn't anyone else hungry?*

He looked toward the other students. Most of them—the ones who weren't exhausted or nursing their injuries—looked intensely interested in the match to come.

*…It's not gonna be any fun to watch, guys*, he thought, looking at them.

Then the booing began.

"Let the Empress kick your ass, already!" came a shout from the crowd. Blade guessed it was the guy whose ass had received a thorough kicking from Earnest in the second round. *So that's what they want to see.*

"All right, all right. I'll do it..." Resigned to his fate, Blade turned back toward Earnest. "...But are you gonna be okay? You look exhausted."

Earnest was still sweating profusely. Her forehead was soaked. She looked ill; despite all this strenuous exercise, she was more pallid than flushed.

"Are you really sure about this?" Blade approached her. He reached out his hand and attempted to touch her forehead.

"Shut up!"

Earnest's sword whizzed through the air. Blade nimbly pulled his hand back. If he hadn't, it really *would* have been amputated just now—cleanly, too, right at the wrist joint.

"I'm fine... Let's do it... You can't get out of this!"

Earnest kept her sword fixed on him, murderous rage clear in her voice. Blade, left with no other choice, faced her.

He readied his sword across from her in the middle of the arena. But Earnest was clearly starting to grow weak. He watched her, still unsure what to do...and then she began to stagger.

"...Whoa!"

Instantly, he ran up to his opponent, catching her in his arms before she hit the ground.

"Hey, don't pass out on me—*hey!*"

But it was too late. Earnest was unconscious. The crowd began to murmur.

"Did you see it?"

"I couldn't see anything..."

"Where's the nurse's office?!" Blade shouted, hefting up Earnest's body. She looked thin and light, but she was actually pretty heavy. Muscular.

The audience parted for him as he left for the nurse's office, carrying her. How did the match end, you ask? It was called off, of course.

## ○ Scene XIII: The Nurse's Office

"Sorry, magic's outside my realm of expertise."

After examining Earnest, the doctor wasted no time offering this conclusion. Blade glared at her, but his attempt at staring her down was thoroughly blocked by her thick chest armor.

Blade had known this doctor for a long time. Just recently, they had spent months together, though that was because she had led the medical team that nursed him back to health after he fought the Overlord. She was here at this school thanks to the king's machinations, no doubt. She'd normally be extremely overqualified for a school nurse position. Her advanced medical skills had an almost eerie, taboo quality to them—she could heal any injury or illness, it was said, so long as you weren't dead yet.

"Magic?" Blade asked. "...Is *that* what this is? What kind?"

"Like I said, I wouldn't know, all right?"

That wasn't good. Earnest wasn't suffering from simple exhaustion or injury. This was going to be much more difficult to treat.

"If she were hurt or sick," said the doctor as she scribbled notes on a clipboard, "I could handle that, whether she was dead or not. But I'm useless with magic. You'll need to track down some sort of specialist."

Correction—death didn't stop her, either, it seemed.

"But...here, take this off," she continued.

"H-hey!" Blade drew back as the doctor placed her hands on his shirt.

She licked her bright red lips...as she rubbed her body up against his. "I just want to look at your scars, you know... Or did you want me to do *that* for you, too?"

"What do you mean...'that'?"

"Hmm. You've become a fine young man, haven't you? Once upon a time, you were a thirteen-year-old kid, well out of my range...but now, maybe it'd be fine, wouldn't it?"

She ran a finger up his chest. What did she mean by "out of range" or "fine"? Blade had no idea. He was pretty ignorant about that sort of thing—and most other "normal" things, too.

"All right, playtime's over. Undress before I have to rip those clothes off you."

The doctor turned away, though not before tracing a few more letters of the alphabet on his chest. No longer feeling her warmth against his skin was a relief, but also a bit of a disappointment.

Blade meekly followed her instructions. He owed her his life, after all.

Removing his shirt revealed the many scars on his upper body—a countless number—some old, some new, some from his Hero days, some given to him by the Overlord himself.

"Looks like the healing process is going quite well," the doctor said, running her hands (this time in a way more befitting of a doctor) across his wounds. "But you still can't afford to overdo it... If you try to do even thirty percent of what you did in your glory days, you really *will* die this time, do you understand?"

"I won't, trust me. I don't need to. I'm a regular person now, okay?"

Blade pulled at some of his bangs as he pleaded with the doctor. In the aftermath of losing his Hero powers, the right half of his hair had turned pure white.

"You think *this* will ever go back to normal?"

"Push it, and you'll go bald next time."

"B-bald?"

They were interrupted by a groan from Earnest. Blade, freeing himself from the beautiful doctor's fingers, hurriedly put his shirt back on.

"...Where am I?" Earnest looked up at the ceiling, then at the faces of Blade and the doctor.

"You passed out on the Proving Ground," said Blade. "Don't you remember?"

"I did? I..." Suddenly, the haze cleared from her expression. "...Oh no!"

She tried to get up, but Blade stopped her and placed her back into bed.

"Did I...um...do something really terrible, or...?"

"Terrible? No, not really. We had just started our match, and then you fell down out of nowhere."

"Just fell? ...Oh. Well...that's good."

Why did she sound relieved? What was she worried about? Blade had no way of knowing.

"But I *did* have a terrible time bringing you over here," he said.

It took a good ten seconds for Earnest to understand what he meant.

"Damn it, I'm... I'm not *that* heavy..."

"Get some rest, okay?"

The doctor brought a hand to her forehead, speaking softly as if comforting a child before bedtime. This came as a surprise to Blade. He didn't know she was capable of such a tone.

"I'll call for a sorcery instructor. I'm not sure if this is a curse or what, but your—"

"Stop, please." Earnest's voice was just as stern as her face. Her eyes, nearly closed a moment ago, were now narrow and sharp.

"Listen, I'm a doctor, and you need to—"

"I...I asked you to stop, please."

Earnest pointed the sword in her hand at the doctor. She had never let go of it, even while unconscious—or rather, the sword had refused to leave her hand, like it was glued to her palm.

"I'm perfectly fine now," Earnest continued.

She tried to get up, but she was still wobbling.

"Don't push yourself. Rest here a little longer."

Blade knew this doctor well. A patient pointing a sword at her wasn't about to make her lose her cool. She could perform surgery in the middle of a dragon's lair. One icy glare from her would make an Ancient Dragon run for the hills.

"Move," said Earnest.

"I refuse," said the doctor.

Neither of them were giving an inch. Blade, who knew both of them, was sure they'd never relent.

"Well...," said Blade. "Don't you think it's all right...Doctor?"

"Did you just call me 'Doctor'?"

Her beautiful eyebrows shot up, and she stared at him. Her glare could make an Ancient Dragon cry, but Blade persevered.

"She—Earnest—is fine now, I think. Can't you let her go?"

The doctor kept staring at him. Blade would need a stronger case.

"I'll take over for you," he said.

"I'm going to hold you to that."

And so, with what sounded like a "normal" conversation on the surface, Earnest was freed from the nurse's office.

"I can walk by myself," she said.

Earnest was using her sword's scabbard as a cane, while Blade held her arm, deep in thought. Only he and the doctor knew the meaning of the "promise" they had just made. "I'll take over for you" was code for *I'll take full responsibility for whatever happens.*

"Hey...don't tell anyone about this, all right?" Earnest, despite what she'd said, was still grabbing onto Blade for support.

"About what?"

"...If you don't know, then fine."

Blade did know, but he pretended not to.

Just what did Earnest think she might have done while unconscious?

## ○ Scene XIV: Royal Forbidden Library

Blade was walking down an old, timeworn hall, twirling the key he had received from the king in his fingers. It was a strange key, made of some kind of transparent crystal. It had taken a carefully balanced mix of threats, cajoling, and flattery to get it, and it led him to a certain storage room below the palace—one called the "Royal Forbidden Library." Most people didn't know it existed, but those who did knew well what it was for. Beneath the place was a large, mysterious structure. The whole capital, in fact, had been built atop it.

Blade descended a hidden stairwell from the first floor. Very few people had ventured into this area of the palace. At a certain depth, the walls and ceiling clearly became something from another generation, progressing from stone to an oddly smooth, jointless surface.

"Guess I don't need this anymore."

Blade put his hand around the ball of light he was using for illumination, crushing it. The spell was intro-level magic, something that any conjurer could cast, and Blade was fairly skilled. That said, he rarely had the chance to use his magic, since stabbing and slashing often got the job done faster.

Despite losing this light, he wasn't shrouded in darkness. The walls down here emitted a dim natural glow, lighting the way as Blade progressed toward his destination.

"Ready, set... Go!"

Blade let loose the move he had been charging up.

This skill belonged not to the dragon-destroyer group, but to another skill family. He didn't want to wreck the hallway, and damaging the storage room was out of the question. No, he needed a different type of skill to fight this Guardian—a thin beam of highly honed energy would do the trick.

The ancient Guardian he was facing kept watch over the storage room. It would usually just stand there, unless you went out of your way to approach it. There were rumors that it had been on the job for thousands of years, but the truth was unclear.

Launching a skill as Blade had just done would, of course, trigger its "enemy detected" routine and cause it to start attacking, but—

"...Right."

Blade looked at the half-destroyed Guardian for a moment, then nodded. Sparks flew out from the crevices in its silver armor, and bits of metallic fiber were starting to show. It was already repairing itself, the cracks in its single eyeball filling in before Blade's eyes. He had maybe ten or so minutes before the Guardian would be operational again. He could have wrecked it more, perhaps, but that would require skills that could damage the hall and its rooms.

There was a hexagonal keyhole to one side of the storage room door. When Blade inserted the crystal key into it, the door soundlessly opened.

Inside, he was a greeted with a view unlike any other. Light, neither magical nor from a lamp, filled the chamber. It illuminated a multitude of things, many of which had uses Blade could only guess at. He could recognize basic stuff, like the desks and chairs, but even those were strange. One chair was shaped like a giant egg, enveloping anyone who sat in it. The table in front of it had no flat surface at all, making it impossible to place anything on it.

A crystalline panel was set into its surface, and as Blade looked around the room, he found more of these panels on all four walls. Not a single book could be found, but this was a library nonetheless.

A total of ten chairs were inside the room, though many of them were broken or had nonfunctional crystal panels. Only two or three of them worked, and Blade sat down at one of these. Using his crystal key one more time, he activated the panel on the desk.

"Okay…"

He brought both of his hands up, waving them around. The flat crystal panel filled up with a type of magical runic language. This was a lost written script from ancient times; not even Blade could read more than a few words of it. But a self-styled "great sorcerer" he knew had taught him a little trick for things like this. He tapped a certain part of the panel with his fingers, and the script transformed into modern language before his eyes.

"Um… Magic items…Weapons…and…here we go, Swords."

He began scanning through the table of contents, going from Magic Items to Weapons and finally Swords. A long list of sword names scrolled by—famed magical blades, renowned holy swords. Blade had the chance to use a few of these during his old Hero days.

This was why they called this room the Royal Forbidden Library. Every kind of information imaginable could be found here.

"Oh… Wait, I don't know it, do I?"

But the name of the magic sword on Blade's mind right now was a mystery. Searching for swords associated with flames brought up a list a mile long; it took him three seconds to give up on that approach. He then decided to try something else.

"Kingdom…training school…student…sort by name… Earnest."

The panel produced a wealth of information about his classmate. He tried to avoid peeking at anything too personal as he searched for details about her sword.

"Hmm… The 'magic sword Asmodeus,' huh? Sounds like a monster."

But just as Blade began reading, he heard an ominous *creeeeak-clank, creeeeak-clank*. The Guardian was half-rebuilt by now, and it was heading his way. It reached out toward Blade with one arm, its single eye glowing red, indicating it was in attack mode. A cylindrical pipe could be seen in its hand, and light was gathering around the tip.

"Lay off. I just got to the good part."

Blade's arm shot out, unleashing a bolt of energy at the Guardian. Its hulking body made three complete revolutions as it was thrown against the opposite wall.

Now Blade could absorb himself in this Asmodeus stuff.

"…Hmm," he said thoughtfully after a while. He now understood what had happened to Earnest. He had the information he'd set out to learn—he knew what the problem was, how to solve it, and everything in between. His business in the Royal Forbidden Library was complete.

He gathered the Guardian's parts and piled them up by the entrance so it would have an easier time repairing itself.

"Sorry about that," he said as he patted its cracked eye. Then he turned and left.

## ○ Scene XV: Earnest

Two or three days passed.

Blade was sitting in a corner of the Proving Ground, making no secret of the fact that he was cutting class as he observed Earnest from a distance. She had been off her game for a few days after the incident, but now she was finally getting in some exercise.

She had placed four attack automatons around her in each direction of the compass and was training for multitarget battles. She slashed down one of them and dodged the attack of a second in a single move. Then she swiped at this second target, taking advantage of the fact that the fourth was blocked from attacking by the third.

*Yep. Fundamental stuff for multitarget battles.*

Even fighting three or more foes at once, if you ensure that every move you make is both an attack and an evasion, you can fight much the same as you would against two opponents. You don't need to outclass them that much to pull it off, either. When Blade was around six years old, he was thrown into an Ancient Dragon's lair. Surrounded by more dragons than he could count, he had learned this strategy. The hard way.

*…How nice of them to teach it in school. I'm a little jealous.*

Earnest had devised this training method herself. Once she tested it out, she'd no doubt be teaching it to the other students. The senior class didn't have any instructor—well, okay, there was one assigned, but all he did during class was stand at the far end of the arena and make himself as small as possible. Earnest alone decided how the class would train.

Blade had been looking for the right opportunity to speak with her since the day of their tournament. He had the sneaking suspicion she was trying to avoid him. When he tried to make eye contact, she'd turn away. When he said hello, she wouldn't respond. They still shared a table in the dining hall, but she'd finish her meal quickly and leave in a hurry. And given how Claire shook her head wildly when he asked about it, he was pretty sure this was more than just his imagination.

Before, he probably would have agonized over whether she hated him, or had stopped being his friend, or whatever. But Blade wasn't even slightly fazed. After all, he knew the reason for her behavior.

"Earnest." He finally tried addressing her while she was taking a break from training and wiping the sweat off her brow. "I wanted to talk."

"Wh-what?"

Earnest held her towel against her chest, in full self-defense mode. Blade found it hard to continue. Did she really fear him that much?

"Ummm..."

This came as something of a shock. His mind went blank, and he strained to recall what he was trying to tell her.

"Uhhh... Do...do you think we could go someplace to talk alone?"

"Huh? ...What do you want?"

*Glare.* Her eyes were like knives stabbing him. He'd experienced this sensation countless times now, and he was building up a decent immunity.

"I'd like to talk with you," he said.

"Well, it doesn't seem like you want to try something dirty...so what *do* you want?"

"Huh? Dirty...? Like what?"

"Are you threatening me?"

"What?"

"I appreciate you keeping quiet about *that*. But if you think you can blackmail me over it...I'll slash you in two."

*Glare.* She placed a hand on her sword hilt.

"Wait, wait, wait! What do you mean, 'blackmail'? I don't know what you're talking about."

Blade panicked, waving his hands to block her dubious gaze. What was her deal? He didn't know what she meant by "something dirty," either, but *this* made even less sense. What was he supposed to be blackmailing her over, exactly? And why would he do such a thing?

"Like I said, I'm talking about...*that*."

Blade knew what "that" was. It was the thing Earnest was so worried about. She was anxious over what she might have done while unconscious. The answer was "nothing," of course; she passed out, and that was it. She had looked greatly relieved when he told her as much, and after doing his research, Blade now knew what she was so afraid of.

"But why would I blackmail you?" he asked.

"Why not? You've got something you can use against me, don't you? You know I'm the next leader of the Flaming clan..."

"Oh?"

That piece of information wasn't very prominent in Blade's mind. In fact, this was the first time he had heard about it.

"And what being the next leader means..."

Before Earnest could spell it out for him, Blade cut her off.

"It means you're the 'possessor' of that sword, right?"

The Flaming family enjoyed a place among the nobility because many generations ago, a clan member had used that sword in the service of the kingdom. They subsequently evolved into a military clan, serving the king from generation to generation. If Earnest was in possession of the sword, it meant she'd eventually become the family head, skipping her parents' generation entirely.

Blade looked at the magic sword she always kept by her side, and she shot him a puzzled look.

"I knew it," she said. "You're after something, aren't you?"

"I'm not after anything."

"I know what it is. You want my position as head of the class, don't you? Were you hoping to settle our unfinished business from before?"

"What business?" And what did "head of the class" mean here?

"W-well, fine. I-I'll take you on. No matter how strong you are, I know I can—"

"No, I mean, *what* business?" He really didn't know what this was about at all.

"I mean our duel! The tournament final! We never actually fought, did we?"

"Oh. It's fine. That doesn't matter."

He'd finally figured it out. No wonder he'd forgotten. He recalled what "head of the class" meant, too—her position as number-one student at the school. Blade had no interest in that. If she wanted to be king of the mountain, she could go right ahead.

"After all, if you beat me, you'll become the new head of the class, and—Wait, what? Did you just say it 'doesn't matter'?"

"Yeah. I don't really care."

Blade was here at school to enjoy his post-Hero life as a normal person.

Whether he was head of the class, number two, or dead last in the rankings, he didn't care.

"I'm much more interested in you," he said.

"Huh? Wait, um..."

Blade scoped out their surroundings. A few students were training a little ways away. There were things he wanted to discuss with her, but he didn't want to do it here.

"Let's go somewhere we can talk privately," he said, trying to look as serious as possible.

Earnest took a moment to consider this.

"W-well, then... Let's go to my room." She stood up and began walking. Before leaving the arena, she shouted at the other students, "Everyone, keep up with your current training!"

"Um...? Earnest...? Where are you going?" The class instructor, stationed by the Proving Ground entrance, stopped her.

"I'm leaving early," she replied, her tone clear and firm.

## ○ Scene XVI: Earnest's Room

Blade was now in Earnest's quarters.

"Listen up," she said, "don't get the wrong idea about this. You're nothing more than a friend to me."

"Okay."

What idea *should* he have about this? It was true that Earnest was his friend, but... Actually, this was the first time she had used the word *friend* to describe him. That made him a little happy.

"I only invited you to my room because we have secret things to talk about. There's not even a shred of other motivation at work here, okay?"

"Okay."

*Other motivations? Like what?* Going somewhere more private was his suggestion in the first place.

"I did say I'd be your friend...but if you push your luck, I have ideas of what I could do to you—"

"Ummm, can we cut to the chase?"

Blade cut Earnest off, too exhausted to keep playing along. Earnest, to his surprise, was kind enough to simply nod.

"So I'm gonna get right down to business. Are you ready?"

Another nod.

"Okay... I know the secret behind that sword."

"How...much do you know?"

"Pretty much all of it, I think."

Assuming the Royal Forbidden Library hadn't skipped any details, he knew everything. To start, Blade decided to tell her what he had learned.

"It's a magic sword with its own will and intelligence. It selects its own wielder, and it can provide massive power to whoever it accepts. You are its official possessor, but your relationship isn't complete. You aren't able to access its full powers yet. And if you can't tap into all of it, that proves that you aren't in complete possession of it."

He kept an eye on Earnest's face as he revealed what he knew. He wasn't looking to verify the truth of what he was saying, though. The Royal Forbidden Library told no lies. That said, it hadn't recorded *her* take on the situation—and he was gauging her response to find out how she felt about those truths.

Earnest nodded slightly. "The magic sword Asmodeus...was kept in storage for a very long time after its previous possessor died. I was pretty stupid, I guess. I knew our family had this famous sword, and I wanted a look at it... I begged for it as my birthday present, but my family said no... So in the middle of the night, I took the key to my father's study and sneaked in to see the sword—the famed sword my ancestors had used...the legendary blade that made the Flaming clan renowned as one of the 'four swords offered to the king,' and all that. But I had no idea that it wasn't just a famous sword, but a magic one...and that it had a curse."

Her eyes were fixed upon some point in the distance.

"So I opened up the glass case, and the moment I touched it, the sword's will transferred itself into me. This sword *is* cursed. It craves blood and massacre. It bides its time, always waiting for a chance to rip everything apart and burn it all down. And yes, my ancestors served as its possessors. They had the self-control to do so responsibly—to suppress the sword's will. They used it for its power alone...so they could do what was right with it."

Blade nodded back at Earnest. This gave her the courage to continue.

"And I am *so* proud of my ancestors. Not once did they allow the sword's curse to spread across the land. But I wasn't up to the task. I was too young. And when the sword's will flooded into me..." Earnest clutched at her chest. "I nearly died. I had a terrible fever and straddled the line between life and death for days. The sword tried to take over my body..."

The Royal Forbidden Library records stated that when the magic sword Asmodeus recognized someone as its possessor, it would unleash astounding power—but if it refused someone, it would turn them into a crazed, bloodthirsty monster.

"But that didn't happen," said Blade.

"No. The magic sword hasn't recognized me as its possessor. Normally, you're supposed to make the attempt only after you prepare yourself. You need mental training—full control over your body, your technique, and your mind. You need to build up the traits of a champion." She looked mystified as she continued. "But as you can see, it still hasn't taken me over. Why, I wonder?"

"You're just too stubborn."

She must have taken that as a joke, because she laughed. She reached behind her head, removing her hair clip and letting her hair flow down her back.

"Look at my hair. Pretty red, isn't it?"

"Yeah."

"I used to have black hair," she said, caressing it. "From my mother's side. But after seven days on the verge of death, it became this fiery red color. Apparently, this has only happened once before, to the very first possessor of the sword. So maybe it likes me after all. And when I let my guard down...I can hear it. It keeps saying 'I want to slice' and 'Let me taste blood' and 'Let me burn it all.' I hear it in Asmodeus's own voice."

She was constantly fighting. Fighting against the fear that she would someday become a blood-crazed murderer. The Royal Forbidden Library records had explained that the strength of her will was what kept the magic sword from invading her mind.

"As long as I don't tap into the magic sword's power, it's not actually that hard on me. But earlier…you know, I used too much of it. Sophie was a big challenge."

"How old were you?" Blade asked.

"Huh?"

"How long have you been…?"

"It happened on the night of my sixth birthday."

*She's been fighting alone for over ten years. That has to be enough, right?* And the library had offered one possible way to fundamentally solve her problem.

"Earnest… You have been accepted by the magic sword as its partial possessor. But it's after your life. It's always looking for an opening to sink its teeth into you."

"I know. But it's all right. I try not to use its power too much…and, you know, as long as I'm careful and don't create an opening like before—"

"There's a way out, you know."

There was a solution. She would need to face off against the magic sword again—and this time, she had to make it fully accept her as its possessor. If she did that…

"I know," she said, her voice as firm as her expression. "But I can't. What if I fail? There would be a murderer loose in the world, carrying Asmodeus, like a demon thirsting for blood and—"

"It'll be all right," Blade said.

"Oh, don't try to comfort me. You're being irresponsible. And besides, I'm the one who'll have to fight it—"

It seemed his message wasn't getting across to her, so Blade decided to try one more time. He made his expression and tone as clear as possible.

"It'll be all right. I'll cut you down if I have to."

"...? Huh?" Earnest blinked several times as she looked at him. "Um...?"

"I'll cut you down," he repeated. If she dueled her own sword, lost, and was taken over...he'd cut her down. He'd settle things for her. That was why it would be all right.

"But you...," she started.

"You think I can't do it?" Blade asked with a grin.

"No, I think you can," Earnest replied with a grin of her own.

"So what's the problem, then?"

"No problem."

She seemed oddly cheerful as she spoke.

## ○ Scene XVII: Late Night

Late at night, the two of them were all alone on the Proving Ground.

They had decided to go through with their plan that very night. Waiting wouldn't change anything, and if they didn't do it now, they likely wouldn't do it later. And besides, if they had it in themselves to do it later, they might as well do it now. Earnest and Blade felt the same way and had thus opted to do things right away.

For the time, they had chosen midnight. They would carry out their task at the Proving Ground, in preparation for what might come *afterward*. Blade had brought along his favorite sword. His old one from his Hero days had been lost when he faced off against the Overlord. This was only a backup sword, but he loved it nonetheless.

"I washed up thoroughly, so...," Earnest said as soon as she arrived.

"Mmm?" Blade wasn't sure what she meant.

"My body, I mean."

"Mmm?"

He understood her answer, but he couldn't fathom why she had bothered. He didn't dwell on it, though. He knew that in the eastern lands, there was something called *misogi*, a purification ceremony using water that one undertook before important occasions.

"I believe in you, all right?" he said. "I know you'll beat that sword."

"And I believe in you. If something happens, I know you'll take care of things."

"You got it."

"Yes. Just you wait."

The two of them exchanged smiles. Considering what was about to unfold, Earnest didn't seem at all nervous. Being so relaxed just before a life-and-death struggle was something even seasoned warriors found difficult. Blade was impressed.

Earnest walked toward the center of the arena, her weapon at her side. The battle against her magic sword would be a mental one, and Blade couldn't help with that. All he could do was watch.

When she reached her destination, Earnest unsheathed her sword, holding it up vertically.

"Magic sword Asmodeus! I, Earnest Flaming, seek to forge a pact with you." She stared straight at the blade, her voice clear as she issued the challenge. "Obey the ancient covenant, and welcome me inside of you. Welcome me in, and test me. Just *try* to consume me!"

And with that—

*"Very well."*

—a voice sounded from nowhere—a pure expression of will, not of sound. Whirling fire surrounded the scene. The sword's flames formed columns shooting up from the ground.

Earnest's body was swallowed up by the flaming tornado. Blade saw it all happen from up close, not moving an inch as he watched. He was in shock. He had seen swords with their own will before, but never one that talked.

His sword was out of its scabbard, ready for use at any time, as he continued to watch the flaming whirl, his face lit red by its light.

## ○ Scene XVIII: Earnest's Trial

Earnest was now in the world inside her mind. There, she was nothing but a naked little girl. A massive presence loomed before her—she perceived it as a giant with a body made of searing lava.

"You must be Asmodeus."

"I am."

"I'll get straight to the point. You must submit to me."

"*I refuse,*" the flame giant said. "*I was created to slash. To destroy. To burn.*"

"I won't let you. Not as long as my family possesses you."

"*Yes. I have been constrained for hundreds of years.*"

"So I guess you're not gonna do what I say?"

"*Of course not.*"

"How about we make a deal? I'll let you slash and destroy and burn…but only when I deem it necessary."

"*I was created to destroy all.*"

"No. I decide what gets destroyed. To protect what needs to be protected. You are nothing but a force. Whether you are a force for good or for evil—that is for me to decide."

"*You are young. I could easily overpower you.*"

This voiceless expression of will earned a smirk from Earnest. *"All right. You're a man, aren't you?"*

"*I have no sex.*"

*Yeah right,* thought Earnest. *Only a man would bluff so brazenly. This guy is falling over himself trying to claim he can crush me. Definitely a man.*

"Ha-ha-ha-ha!" Earnest laughed. She knew how to laugh in just the right tone to deliver the most damage possible to her instructors. When she laughed at them like this, they would immediately lose their cool—

"*I am fire! I am strength! I am pure violence, lording over every type of destruction!*"

*See? Too easy.*

"Enough talk! Come at me!" Earnest roared.

She wasn't going to waste any more time. The giant's body transformed

into flame, and so did Earnest. They spiraled around each other, intermixing as they rose higher and higher. Soon, it was impossible to tell them apart. They had formed one single, undulating pillar of fire.

## ○ Scene XIX: Confrontation

The border between her and not-her was starting to blur. *Who am I?* It became less and less clear.

*Destroy. Destroy. Destroy. Slash. Slash. Slash. Burn. Burn. Burn.*
Intense impulses sprang forth.
*No. No. No. Don't do it. Don't do it. Don't do it. I would never.*
Trying to hold these impulses back was a challenge. *Which one is the real me?* She felt like she could choose between either of them. But what was the right choice? Destruction sounded like fun. *Destroy. Slash. Burn… Ahh, that probably feels really great.* Holding back was tough, painful. *Why am I holding back anyway?*

She felt like she had been holding herself back forever. Wasn't it about time she let loose for a change? All her life, she had been surrounded by things she could have destroyed at any time. She kept from destroying those things, and those people, only through sheer force of will.

*Why am I holding myself back? For my clan? My friends? I don't have any. No, wait, I have one. I made one just recently. And thanks to him, I'm able to fight right now.*

What she'd feared was the aftermath. Only she could fight against her magic sword. If she lost, it was all over. She'd become an uncontrollable monster, wandering the land and killing countless people. That frightened her. She was so scared of the worst possible outcome that she had settled for a path only one step away from it. She couldn't afford to fail, and that had prevented her from taking this challenge as well. That's how it always was, until he came along. He'd given her the words she needed most.

"I'll cut you down."

It was okay to fail now. She was allowed to lose. If worse came to worst, he would put an end to everything.

*And that's why I'm fighting. Yes. Let's fight.*
*...Fight? Fight what? ...These impulses.*
*Why am I fighting? ...Because I decided to.*
*"I"? Which "I" is this? This captive who can't destroy anything without a possessor? Or this prisoner bound by her clan, bound by her ethics, bound by her reputation and honor, bound by everything in her life?*
*Either way, I'm tied down. So does it really matter which one I choose...?*
*...I'm tied down? Who? Me?*
*No. I chose this myself. This is my pride. My...my... I...*
*I...I...*
*I...am Earnest...*
*...Earnest Flaming!*

She shouted out her own name, screaming it as proudly as she could.

## ○ Scene XX: Flame Empress

Holding up his unsheathed sword, Blade watched, unblinking.

Scorching flame was everywhere, and Earnest was inside of it. It kept burning, minute after minute, as she continued to fight.

Ever so slowly, the column of fire began to change. The flames flickered, growing wilder and more unstable. Blade steadied his grip on his sword.

Suddenly, the fire burned out, disappearing in an instant and leaving no trace behind. The girl with the fiery red hair was floating above the arena, her feet slowly coming back to the ground. She staggered.

Blade instantly closed the distance, catching her naked body in his arms.

Earnest looked weakly back at him. She was exhausted to the core, but there was no insanity evident in her eyes.

"I...I'm back," she said.

"Yeah... Welcome back."

She smiled, then shut her eyes once more. Supporting her with one arm, Blade used the other to sheathe his sword. There was no need for it now.

## Chapter 2:
# Sophie

○ **Scene I: The Usual Drills**

They were on the Proving Ground as usual—a typical second period.

Blade was seated in one corner of the arena, clearly cutting class. His chin was perched on the handle of his wooden sword as he kept his eyes squarely on Earnest. She was busy talking with three or four other students about effective practice techniques.

Her mood seemed completely different now—in a good way, of course. Before, when people still called her the Empress, though she had a knack for devising excellent training regimens, she tended to force them high-handedly on others. Now she was taking everyone's feedback. No method worked perfectly for every single person, so Earnest would make adjustments to address any problems. The biggest difference of all, however, was the instructor. Once banished to one side of the arena's entrance, he was now joining in the discussion.

"Oh, I see. I didn't think about that." Earnest nodded at the instructor's advice.

It was true that he was the type who wouldn't survive half a day on the front lines. But skill in battle and skill at teaching were two very different things. Even Blade had to admit to that.

"Thank you very much, sir," Earnest told the instructor.

Once upon a time, she had shown respect to the king alone. Now she was even using *sir* with her teachers.

With Earnest so different now, the senior class had changed quite a bit. Before, the Empress had always kept the students on edge during school hours, exuding a nerve-racking aura with every move she made. She seemed to be constantly implying "If you can't even do *this*, you don't deserve to be in the senior class," and no one was immune. She was tough on herself, and that strictness had seeped out and wound up directed at everyone around her. But now that she had defeated Asmodeus and become its complete possessor, she no longer needed to be so harsh on herself. She could afford to be more relaxed—and that, in turn, had positive effects on everyone else.

"Hey. No cutting class," came Earnest's voice.

Only after Blade had already dodged whatever it was she threw at him did he realize what had happened. A short sword was now standing upright, driven deep into the ground.

"Whoa," cried Blade. "What if that hit me?"

"That won't happen," she said honestly as Blade handed her back the sword. She was right, but that was no excuse.

"You know…" Blade looked at Earnest, closely examining her from the top of her forehead to the tips of her feet. "You've really changed."

"Oh? How so?"

Apparently, she had no awareness of it. Blade turned toward the class, hoping they would back him up. Everyone nodded.

"Oh! …Wait, no. It's really not like that…"

Earnest hurriedly ran a hand through her hair. Two or three classmates approached Blade and jabbed him with their elbows suggestively.

"What?"

Blade brushed them aside. Leonard the lancer, however, seemed particularly keen on elbowing him to death.

"Hey, you mind if I spear this guy through? He's so oblivious, he doesn't even notice when a girl changes her hairstyle."

At Leonard's hint, Blade finally realized what was going on.

"Ahhh...ahhh...ahhh."

Blade pointed at Earnest's hair. She used to keep it tied tightly behind her head, but now it was flowing lightly down her back.

*Ohhh! Right! It really did change!*

Earnest had a new hairstyle. No *wonder* she seemed so different! That had to be part of it, right?

"Wh-what do you think?" she asked.

"What do I think?"

Earnest was asking him about something, but he didn't understand what. He stood there, confused, as his classmates kept elbowing him.

"No, really, *what?!*" he asked again.

This elbowing was starting to get old. He picked up his sword, swinging it around and chasing away his attackers. Leonard deftly used his heavy spear to deflect it. Clangs filled the air.

*Oh man. I feel like such a student right now. Being normal sure is nice. This is great.*

"No, I told you—it's not like that," said Earnest. "...Quiet down, all right?"

There was nobody around her; she was talking to herself. Blade was thinking about how weirdly she was acting when he realized she was looking at the sword on her hip. Asmodeus had more than just free will—it could talk, too. Perhaps it was using that power to transmit its will directly into its possessor's brain.

"Hey, Blade..." She stopped Blade's little horseplay session with Leonard. "If you're determined to goof off..."

"I'm not goofing off." He turned toward Earnest while fending off Leonard's high-speed stabs with one hand.

"If you're just playing around," she corrected, "then can you watch her, please?"

"Her?" He followed Earnest's gaze to find a girl clothed in blue at the edge of the Proving Ground. "Oh, Sophie?" There she was, performing some kind of exercise over and over. "Why's she training by herself?"

"It beats a certain *someone* who's not training at all."

"I'm not goofing off!"

The flurry of lance strikes had subsided, and Blade turned toward the dashing young man launching them, only to find him struggling to catch his breath.

"Leonard, your main issue right now is stamina," said Earnest. "Ten-kilometer jog, every day, for the rest of your life, am I clear?"

"The rest of my life? That's kinda…"

The dashing young man seemed about to issue a complaint, but Earnest had already turned away. Her wide-open eyes were focused on Blade now.

"She's always over there, you know," she said. "Training by herself."

Blade looked at Sophie again. Her hands and feet were tracing beautiful arcs in the air as they thudded against the automatic training dummy. She'd been at it this whole time.

"Maybe she'll listen if *you* talk to her."

"Why me?"

"If someone orders her to do something, she'll do it. But *that* was the first time I'd ever seen her do something of her own volition."

"Sorry?"

"You know… When we all first met, you went up to her like an idiot and said, 'I am Blade!' didn't you?"

"'Like an idiot'…?"

Earnest's honest appraisal stung. He vowed to himself that he'd use a different introduction next time.

"If you had ordered her to state her name, she would have. But you didn't do anything like that, and yet she gave her name anyway, right?"

"What, that's all you're talking about?"

"It's a big deal, okay? It was a first."

"Uh-huh."

Apparently, Sophie was a bit strange—or maybe *unique* was a better descriptor.

"If you don't say anything to her, *that's* what she does. She'll do anything you explicitly ask for, but that's it. I want her to start thinking for herself. She needs to learn how to take the initiative."

"Okay. But if *I* tell her to do something, how's that different from you doing it?"

"Try to get around that... I want *you* to figure this out, okay? ♡"

With a quick wink, she passed the job off to him. So, without any recourse, Blade walked over to Sophie. To tell the truth, he was happy for the diversion. She was, after all, his friend, and friends help friends out.

"Hey!" He raised a hand at Sophie, who was still busy training. "I am Blade!"

"I know," she replied, expression as cool as her voice.

*Wait, no! We're already past that!*

"Ummm. Earnest asked me to watch you...while you train."

*Crap! I messed up again!*

He wasn't doing this because he was told to. He was doing it because she was his friend. *I totally failed.*

"Is that an order?" Sophie asked, raising one eyebrow a little but otherwise looking totally unaffected. It was impossible to tell what she was thinking. He had already messed up once—he couldn't afford another error. As he thought this—

"N-no, uh..." *Wh-what's going on? It's like the words are stuck in my throat.* "I mean, you...um, it's like..."

Blade panicked, which only made it harder to speak.

Sophie quietly waited, arms crossed as she stood patiently. She'd probably wait there forever, he realized, until he was able to speak...and that thought made things a lot easier. The words began to flow again.

"No, it's not an order or anything. I just want to help you because we're friends."

He finally got out what he wanted to say—clearly, fully, and correctly.

"This is all I know," she blurted out, raising her fists in front of her.

Blade had assumed she fought barehanded against a swordswoman like Earnest at the tournament because she felt that gave her the best chance to win... But maybe that wasn't the case. It seemed she literally didn't know how to fight with weapons.

"Why do you fight barehanded?" he asked.

"Because this is all I've learned."

The strange replies kept on coming. There were, indeed, more than a few mysterious aspects to Sophie.

"Well, I'll teach you, okay? Maybe we can start with a sword. That should help with the basics."

"I learned that the basics of battle lie in barehanded combat."

"You may be right, but..."

Certainly, you needed to learn how to work your body before you picked up a weapon. If you were totally untrained and someone handed you a sword, you might end up lopping your leg off or something. But this girl clearly had all the physical ability she needed. Unless she had a particular desire to master barehanded combat or something, there was nothing to stop her.

"I'll teach you," Blade said.

"Is that an order?" That same question again.

"Ummm..." He wasn't going to get it wrong a second time.

"An order?" she asked again, looking perfectly serious. This wasn't a joke; she wasn't trying to be obtuse on purpose. *I guess she's just a little awkward,* thought Blade. He might use the same adjective to describe himself, but she was on a whole other level.

"It's not an order. I'm just offering my...support. As a friend."

"It's not an order?"

"No. Not an order. If you don't want to, I won't force you. But I'd like to help with your training... Not a fan?"

She looked troubled at this. He could see confusion on her otherwise-expressionless face. She opened her mouth a couple of times, trying to find the right words...but hesitated each time and closed it again. Blade waited for her to take the initiative. She had done it once before, and he was prepared to wait forever if that's what it took.

After a long while, she finally found the words.

"I...don't mind."

"Okay, it's settled, then. First off—"

He handed her his wooden practice sword. But before he could finish his thought, the bell rang, signifying the end of the period.

"Awww..."

Blade grinned at her as their eyes met. Sophie looked as unaffected as ever, but he thought he could see the traces of a smile on her lips.

*Ah. So she can smile.*

## ○ Scene II: After-School Practice

"Yo!"

On the Proving Ground after school, Blade found a blue figure and waved. The figure looked at him, but she neither waved back nor smiled. All she did was stare at him.

Blade, not quite sure when he should stop waving and put his arm down, opted instead to keep it straight up in the air as he walked toward her.

"I am Blade!"

"I know."

She responded once again, exactly as she had before. That, at long last, broke the ice enough for him to put his arm down. She gave him a puzzled look as he continued to smile.

Since they missed their chance to train together during class, they had promised to find some time after school instead. He had asked what she was doing, not wanting to keep her from any important errands. He was thoughtful that way—normal, the most normal person ever. "I'm not doing anything," she had responded. Usually, you'd take that to mean that she didn't have any business to attend to...but in her case, she might have intended to stand there, literally doing nothing. The thought was kind of scary.

"What?" she asked, probably because of how long he had been staring at her.

"Nothing." Blade smiled. He was prudent enough not to reveal every potentially rude thought on his mind. He was, after all, a normal human man. "Okay. We'll start with the sword, like I promised."

He had two wooden practice swords with him. He gave one of them to Sophie.

Before, the senior class had been using their actual, bladed swords on a pretty much constant basis. As far as Blade knew, though, even the most elite knights used dulled swords during practice. Earnest's students, in other words, had been taking their training even further.

Now that Earnest had, well, chilled out a bit, she was able to make the common-sense judgment that this was more dangerous than useful. She even chose to forego dulled blades, going straight to average wooden practice swords. Hit someone with one of these, and all it did was hurt. A dulled metal weapon couldn't slice, but it could still break bones.

In Blade's view, while magic sentient swords and rocket-powered spears were a bit much, it seemed fine to use dulled blades as knights did. But if someone told him that wooden swords were the "normal" way to go, he had no way to refute that. He had come to understand in recent days that he didn't really know what "normal" was anyway.

"Let's begin with your grip," Blade said, noticing the amateurish way Sophie was holding the sword. He didn't laugh at her, however. If you'd never held a sword before, it was only natural to not know the right way to do it.

"You don't need to squeeze it with all your force. Tense up your little fingers, yes, but the other ones don't need to do much more than wrap around the handle. You won't have free control over it otherwise... Like this."

Blade took up Sophie's wrist, moving it around like a magic wand.

"This?" Sophie got the idea on her first try. All at once, her grip was perfect.

Blade kept going. He taught her how to swing, the proper stance, the basic motions—slashing, slicing, sweeping, stabbing, and so on. The main difference between swordplay and fighting with your fists was that instead of your hands and feet, you were moving an object that weighed several pounds. The wooden swords Earnest devised for their training had a lead core, designed to provide the same heft and balance as the real thing.

Sophie was a quick learner. She would always mess up on her first try. Blade would give her some pointers, explaining what went wrong as he gave a visual demonstration. Then, like clockwork, she'd nail it on the second go. It made for a very constructive session. He thought they must have spent one or two hours at it, but the next time he looked at the clock, four hours had passed.

"Oh crap…" He might've missed his window for dinner at the dining hall by now. "How about we wrap it up for today?"

"Oh," she said.

It was then that Blade realized she wasn't wiping any sweat from her brow. She didn't need to. Blade was sweating a lot more, having worked much harder demonstrating all the moves.

"I think you know your way around a sword well enough by now," he said, giving his stamp of approval. In such a short time—well, four hours, but still—she had already attained a level of competence suited for actual battle.

"Can I beat her now?" she asked.

"Huh? Who do you mean, 'her'?"

"Earnest."

"Oh… I dunno about that…"

Earnest had been practicing almost since birth. She was the result of above-average talent combined with exceptional dedication. No matter how quick a learner Sophie was, it'd likely take years for her to reach a similar skill level. Besides, Earnest had that sword—the magic sword Asmodeus. She had built up a bantering, back-and-forth sort of relationship with it of late, which had only made her stronger. When she was serious about winning, not even Blade was all that excited to fight her. He was supposed to be rehabilitating, not fighting for his life.

"Oh," Sophie said, tossing her wooden sword aside.

"Huh? Hey…"

Blade watched the sword clatter to the ground—and then he was struck by a sweeping kick. Losing his balance, he fell to the ground, only to be pinned down. His arms were grabbed and his joints targeted. In the space of a few seconds, a good ten or so attacks and parries played out.

Before Blade could understand what had happened, Sophie had left him helpless. He had followed his instincts, but somewhere along the line, she'd cornered him.

"This is stronger," Sophie said as her small rear end pushed hard against Blade's stomach.

Blade had to admit she was right. She'd easily pinned him—she was that good. She said it was all she knew, but constantly training at one thing had elevated her technique. Come to think of it, he'd heard she was second only to Earnest in barehanded combat.

"By the way, I can't move…"

"It would be a very poor mount if you could escape it."

"True."

Blade smiled. The mounted position in grappling involved knocking an opponent down, then straddling their body, keeping them still while you went ham with your fists. It gave you an overwhelming advantage while offering your opponent below few means of resistance. There were very few ways to escape it.

"I want you to teach me spear combat tomorrow," she said.

"Sure," Blade replied, unable to resist. He would've agreed even if he wasn't immobilized.

## ○ Scene III: With the King in the Chancellor's Office

"So how is school life treating you?"

Blade had been called into the chancellor's office. The chancellor—or rather, the king—was there, of course. He was seated lazily, head propped up on one arm, behind a gigantic desk that looked like it was carved directly from a ten-thousand-year-old tree. He had a wide, off-putting grin on his face, making Blade wince.

"I really *do* want you to enjoy your time here, you know," he said.

"Then stop calling me out in the middle of class."

"Oh, you were in class? I apologize. I've reached a nice stopping point in my own work, you see."

He had brought his work as king into the chancellor's office. There was a massive amount of it, enough to completely bury all ten thousand tree rings on the desk he sat behind.

"...So what do you think? Anything good happen lately?"

The king looked like an old man eager to hear what his grandson was up to. Blade couldn't frown at him forever.

"I made some friends," he said, his back to the king. Why did he have to report to him about stuff like this?

"That's great..." The king nodded deeply. "You've been acting as a Hero since you were three, after all... Even *I* have close friends, and you... Well, I was hoping coming here would help you make some your age. And it seems you have. Wonderful. I'm very happy."

It was a little frustrating for Blade, but the king sounded genuinely pleased. Blade kept his back turned, feeling vaguely uncomfortable as he stared at a corner of the room.

"...So who are these friends, exactly?" the king continued. "I'll be sure to tell them to be nice to you."

"No way. I'll never tell. Ever." Blade glared at the king. He was going way too far. This was exactly why he hadn't wanted to say anything.

"Well, can you at least tell me if they're boys or girls?"

"Um..."

*Which one was Earnest again?* To tell the truth, Blade was...pretty bad at discerning that sort of thing. He'd assume someone was female due to their long hair, but then it would turn out some men kept theirs long, too. Leonard, for example. And some girls kept theirs short, like Yessica. Sometimes Blade would see someone in a skirt and feel pretty confident they were female, only to find out he'd been completely wrong. It seemed impossible to work out.

In Leonard's case, at least, he had figured it out in short order. The boy kept his shirt mostly unbuttoned, revealing his chest, and it was, well, definitely a man's chest.

*Wait! That's it! I, Blade, have finally discovered a way to tell men and women apart! Yes…and Earnest definitely has fully developed breasts. When I saw her nude earlier, that much was clear. I saw two of them, with little thingies at the ends! And they were pretty large, too!*

"One's a girl."

He felt much more assured now, a smug smile on his face.

"Mmm. Certainly, if you're going to spend time with your classmates, you might as well be getting close to girls. I had quite the busy social calendar when *I* was young, too."

Blade didn't particularly care. "Um…and the others are…a girl, a girl, a boy, a boy…"

Ignoring the king's rambling, Blade employed his newly discovered method to classify all his friends. Just now, he was referring to Claire, Yessica, Clayde, and Kassim, the gang from the junior class.

But what about Sophie? Which one was she? Her hair was relatively short. Her chest area…he wasn't too sure about. And she certainly hadn't been wearing a frilly skirt.

"…and I *think* a girl." He wasn't quite so sure about this claim, but he went with it.

"Who now?"

"Her name is Sophie."

"Ahhh, *her*, eh?"

Oh, come to think of it, didn't Earnest refer to her as, "that girl" and "she" all the time, too? Right. If he had trouble making a call, he could rely on some of those cues, too. He just had to pay attention to the pronouns other people used, and he could figure it out. Blade patted himself on the back.

"Is she the type you like, then?"

"Type?"

"Personally, I recommend a nice hourglass figure, if you know what I mean. Not that there's anything wrong with a more slender body type, of course. There's no wrong answer, you know? All women are *women*, and that makes all of them equally wonderful. Do you see what I mean?"

"No, not at all."

"But look at you! Taking an interest in *her*, eh? I have to say, that's a tad eye-opening."

"What do you mean?"

"Hmm? You knew when you decided to become friends with her, right?"

"I'm serious. What do you mean?"

"She's a good fighter, isn't she?"

"Yeah. She is." Blade nodded. That was one of her most noteworthy traits.

"I thought you'd have some trouble fitting in with a group of normal people. That's why I had her join the school. She may be the only student here who's *not* dreaming of becoming a Hero someday."

"You forgot about me," Blade mumbled to himself. Besides, the king might be going on about raising the next generation of Heroes at this academy, but that was only a very recent objective. For hundreds of years, this school had merely sought to produce young people capable of becoming future cornerstones of society. Look at the roster of current army generals, and you'll find tons of graduates. Some people out there even called this place the "School for Champions."

"She's a strong one," said the king. "Strong, but still incomplete."

"It looks that way, yeah."

She said that she had only been taught fundamental hand-to-hand combat. But where did she get her instruction? Not at this school, it seemed.

"The goal was superhuman strength, you see. She's only about ten percent of the way, and already you can see what she's packing."

Blade was having trouble understanding the context behind the king's words.

"The aim was for her to surpass even you, once she was finished. If she was to get there, she had to first overcome human limitations, don't you agree?"

"Um, can you tell me what you're going on about?"

"I'm talking about the Manmade Hero Project, of course."

"Huh? Manmade…Hero?"

Blade raised an eyebrow. He wasn't sure where this was going.

"Indeed. A Hero like you… Let's call you a 'natural' Hero. If natural Heroes exist, it follows that we can create the same thing with our own hands. A crazy thought, I know, but a certain group of people believed it. They must have resented the fact that only *our* kingdom lays claim to such powerful Heroes."

"I don't recall you laying claim to me."

"Well, certainly not. I told them as much, but apparently that is how it looked to them. There's nothing I can do about what madmen believe."

"But what do you mean 'natural' and 'manmade'? You can't talk about humans like crops… That's awful."

"Oh, I didn't mean anyone was growing humans like crops…but perhaps that's how *they* saw it. And as for *her* case…"

"What, you mean Sophie?" Blade shot the king a dirty "I'll kill you"–type look. The king took it in stride, casually waving it off with one hand.

"Oh, don't worry. *That* organization has been thoroughly crushed by now. I personally saw to it. No matter what their goals were, I won't abide such inhumane behavior. Besides, we've already got you, and you're enough of a Hero. Don't you agree?"

"How many times do I have to tell you I've retired?"

Despite himself, he had suspected the king of being behind this Manmade Hero Project. How embarrassing. But the king hadn't been very clear, either. If he wasn't the culprit, he should have said so right away.

"There were no Heroes before you…and there will be no Heroes after you, either. Don't you think that's how things should be?"

"Will you stop already?"

The king looked at him, his eyes glittering. It was a good thing that ten-thousand-year-old desk—too wide to jump over—sat between them.

It was said that a Hero always appeared when the times called for one. Blade was one such Hero, but he certainly wasn't the first. Starting with the first Hero on record, he was probably the 128th—only "probably" because the chronicles got sketchier the further back you went.

"Like I said," Blade insisted, leaning back in his chair, "I'm no longer a Hero."

If you only wanted someone really strong, you could find such people anywhere. Blade himself knew several people who were better swordfighters than he was. He knew several better casters, too—not that he used his magic very often these days. He might be the only human to master both the sword *and* the spell book at so high a level, but maybe not. Perhaps someone else just as multitalented was out there somewhere. The world was a big place.

But being strong didn't make you a Hero. Blade had been one since the age of three, back when he was just a weak little kid. He wouldn't even have qualified for this school's junior class. But he was a Hero, because he possessed a Hero's powers. Those powers were gone now, canceled out and destroyed along with the Overlord's powers, which had been much like his own.

Thus, Blade was no longer a Hero, no matter how strong he was. Besides, his doctor had told him to keep his output at 30 percent or below what he'd been doing as a Hero.

"I really am looking forward to your rehabilitation," said the king. "That and seeing your power return."

"Weren't we talking about Sophie?"

"Ah, yes. Her full name is Sophitia Femto."

"And?"

"'Femto' is a word in the ancient language scholars like to use. It means *twelve*. In other words, she is the twelfth version of the girl named Sophitia."

"Wait. You mean...?"

"It's just as you think. Our rivals have been dirtying their hands, dabbling in ancient, forbidden techniques. They looked for suitable candidates, then used them as test subjects in their quest to artificially create a Hero's power. They cloned the original subject, conducted experiments under identical conditions, then 'improved' each one. And *she* was their twelfth test subject."

"Hold on, no, wait a minute…"

Blade held his head. This made no sense to him. It *did*, actually, but—if he was right, he didn't want to hear about it. An artificial…Hero? His mind flashed back to all those harsh, cruel days he'd suffered from age three onward.

"That's what I mean," said the king. "They treated them like objects—test subjects. Those kids didn't get to experience real life at all. When we rescued her and I told her she was free, she replied, 'Is that an order?' I didn't even know how to respond… Is she still like that, even now?"

Blade was confused. Sophie had gone through all that…just so someone could create a Hero? They had stolen people's lives? And that was why she acted the way she did?

*And it's all…my fault? My fault.*

His head began to spin.

"A normal…" He struggled to speak; his throat was parched.

"Pardon?"

"A normal person… What does a normal person my age even do?"

Asking the king was likely a mistake, he thought, but the older man was the only other person in the room.

"Well, I think it's a young man's job to enjoy his greatest years. The springtime of his youth."

"What do you mean, the 'springtime of youth'?"

The concept seemed totally disconnected from Blade's lived experience.

"Hmm… Well, let me tell you a fine tale or two from when I was young… She was beautiful, the kind of girl everybody gave up on because they saw her as unattainable. But I didn't let that bother me. I had no reason to. As the ancients said, you are human and I am human, and we are all equal. If I could add something to that nugget of knowledge—*she* was a woman, and *I* a man, and well…you know what that means. So I spoke to her, and—wait. Where are you going? I'm just getting to the good part."

*This old man is hopeless.*

Blade was done here. He stormed out of the office, seeking answers to the new question in his mind: What was the "springtime of youth," and how did one pass it like a normal person?

## ○ Scene IV: Blade Goes Astray

Flying out of the chancellor's office, Blade made a beeline for the nurse. The doctor was his only other adult acquaintance nearby, and among the adults he knew, she was also one of the saner ones, as hard as that might be to believe.

"Oh? Are you hurt? Who's responsible? Go ahead and take off your clothes. Come on, off they go."

Blade grabbed the doctor's wrists to stop her from unbuttoning his shirt.

"Oh, getting a little rough, aren't we?" She brought her face closer to his. "Well, I don't mind that, either. Want to try tying me up?"

"What's the 'springtime of youth'?"

"Mmm? Finally taking an interest in *that*, huh? Perfect. Just sit back and let me teach you *everything* you need to know."

Her red lips moved like they had a life of their own.

"Wait," said Blade. "Be clear. What's the springtime of youth? How would a normal person pass it?"

"Well, they'd procreate as much as possible, of course."

"I need you to be serious! This is important!"

"Well, of course it is. To elaborate, when an organism reaches the age when it can spawn offspring, that's what it's intended to do. An organism's reason for existing is procreation, so doing just that is totally natural."

"I'm talking about *people*! Not organisms!"

"But human beings are organisms, aren't they? Are you saying they aren't? Well?"

"Huh? Um…uhhh…"

Was that true? Was she right?

"Also, personally, I think it's totally normal to prefer the cowgirl position. But here's the church, saying missionary's the only right way to do it... They're so ridiculously old-fashioned," she said, starting to lock the door behind her.

*She was sounding so plausible at first, too! She almost tricked me! Forget this!*

Giving up on the doctor, Blade stormed out of the nurse's office.

Blade passed Leonard, the dashing lancer, on his way down the hallway.

"Oh, just who I needed!"

"What's up, Blade? Why are you out of breath?"

"Springtime! The springtime of youth! What is it? How do *normal* people tackle it?! *Normal* people! What're we supposed to *do*?!"

"Um... I'm not sure where this is coming from...but if I were in a normal school, rather than this place, I'd no doubt be falling in lov—"

*Forget this.*

Blade stomped away, in search of new answers.

"Ahhh! Claire, Claire!"

"Whoa...?! Agh! Blade! This is the changing room...!"

"Who cares?! None of that matters right now! Tell me! You have to tell me! What's the springtime of youth like for normal people?!"

"Huh? The springtime of...what now?!"

Claire held the clothes she was about to put on closer to her body, trying her hardest to stay decent. Yessica, sitting topless next to her, sized up the situation with an "Oh, dear, dear" look on her face and stifled a laugh.

"Um, look, for now, can you get out of here, Blade? I *know* you're not the sort of boy to do stuff like this."

"I'm not asking for the textbook answer! Save your special theories of relativity for the final exam! I want *your* take! What do *you* think?! What do *you* want to do right now, outside of classwork?!"

"What I want to do…outside of school? Ummm… I'd rather not say."

Claire looked to Yessica, seeking her help. Her friend just smiled, not bothering to hide her breasts. Her eyes were saying "Out with it, come on."

Finally, steeling herself, Claire spoke.

"Um…I'd…look for love, and stuff!"

*Forget this.*

Giving up on Claire, Blade stormed out of the girls' locker room.

"Waaaaaaah! Earrrrrrnesssssssst!"

"Wha—ahhh! What the…?!"

Blade caught Earnest just as she was leaving her room. He didn't stop, pulling her back inside. She'd sworn never to let him in again after last time, but here he was. Not that she'd invited him.

"I didn't wanna turn to you, but I have no other choice!"

"Wha…? Wha?! What's going on?! That's such a rude thing to say!"

"I know full well you have no idea what normal is! But I'm gonna ask you anyway!"

"What're you talking about? Are you trying to make me mad? …I mean, I won't try to pretend I'm normal, but still!"

After years of living under strict discipline, Earnest knew she had missed out on a lot in life. She had started trying plenty of new things lately, hoping to make up for lost time—but having someone point that out right to her face was irritating.

"No, like... Normal! *Normal!* What do people *do*?!"

"Huh? Normal how?"

"You know, normal! A normal way to spend the springtime of youth! I just said that!"

"No you didn't. You didn't say anything like that."

Blade was beside himself with panic—he was not acting normally, even by his own standards.

"Just calm down a little, all right? I'll make some tea."

Earnest closed the door, sat Blade down, and began heating some water. She had a magical device in her room exclusively for that purpose. Something like that would cost a small fortune out on the street. Even she knew that much.

*Yes. I've got this. I know all about "normal."*

Blade, sitting on her bed, started muttering something. His unusual behavior was concerning, but more important to Earnest was the fact he was *sitting on her bed*. It was just as unkempt as when she woke up in it that morning. She hadn't changed the sheets. He might be able to smell her scent on them.

"Here. Some tea."

She pressed a cup to his nose. There were two cubes of sugar in it—the *normal* amount. *See? I know normal. I've totally got this.*

"Oh... Thank you." Blade accepted the cup and took a sip. It seemed to calm him a little.

"...So what did you want to know, exactly? How a normal person spends their youth, you said?"

"Now that I've collected my thoughts, you're clearly the wrong person to ask. I'm sorry. I lost myself there." Blade tried to stand up.

"Wait." Earnest stopped him, scowling. This, she thought, was an affront to her dignity. "So basically, you want to know what a normal teenage life is like?"

"Yeah," Blade said, nodding meekly. The gesture was actually kind of cute.

Normal. Normal. The students here tended not to be all that normal, so she couldn't use them as reference—she needed to think about what a normal citizen would do—a normal teenager. That's what Blade wanted to know.

*"You can just talk about all the things you envied."*

"Shut up."

Her sword was mouthing off again. Earnest snapped at it. *Ugh. When I first talked to it, I didn't expect it to be so vulgar...*

"S-sorry," Blade said.

"Don't be," Earnest replied, realizing Blade's mistake. "I was just talking to myself."

*"Tell him about what all the normal kids were obsessed with. Tell them how jealous you were."*

The sword at her hip received a few choice punches. Blade gave her another funny look. Her cheeks were oddly flushed.

Earnest had envied them. Normal, average young people with normal, average lives and no great expectations of breathtaking heroics in the future.

But what Earnest envied most of all was...

"...Falling in love, I guess?"

"That again?"

"Huh?"

"Claire said the same thing..."

"Oh? She did?"

So he'd been asking other people? Realizing she'd given the same answer as someone else embarrassed her a bit.

"Oh...but when I say 'love,' I'm not talking about anything big and serious, okay? I just mean, like, chatting, or going out, or dressing up nice and going to the theater, or a concert..."

Earnest had never done any of that. She'd never gone out with a friend, male or female. Not even alone, for that matter. Training, discipline, self-control—those were what had occupied her days.

"It's your fault, you know," she said to Asmodeus.

"*I will admit to that.*"

"S-sorry," said Blade.

"I said I was just talking to myself! Just ignore me! Quit apologizing all the time!"

"How would *I* know?" Blade asked dejectedly. Of course he couldn't tell. Only Earnest could hear the voice of Asmodeus.

"But all those things I just said… You know, doing that with a boy—I mean, the opposite sex—that's normal teenage stuff, right?"

"It is…?"

"I…think so…"

Neither of them seemed too sure, but they nodded at each other anyway.

"Oh… So that's how it is, huh…? The king, the doctor, Leonard, Claire… They all said the same thing. And you did, too…"

"Huh? The king? Leonard? *Leonard* said the same thing? Oh, I don't like *that* at all…"

"I know about that stuff, though. It's called a 'date,' right?"

"Huh? Um…yes…you could say that."

"Great! Now it all makes sense!"

"No, but… It's not like dating is the only thing young people do… Hey, are you listening to me?"

"I've got it! I've finally got it! Thanks a lot, Earnest! Now I'm really glad I talked to you!"

He shook both of her hands, swinging them up and down.

"Ah, ah-ha-ha-ha-ha… Y-you're welcome!" she said, a stiff smile spreading across her face.

\*

"Sophie! Sophie! Sophie, where are you?"

Blade banged on the door until a girl in her sleepwear peeked out.

"Sophie's in the shower room right now—"

"Thanks!"

Blade took off, zooming toward the shower room. Only very special dorm rooms, like Blade's and Earnest's, came with their own bath and toilet and cooking equipment. Even the other students in the senior class had to make do with common spaces.

Since time was of the essence, Blade decided to skip knocking. He threw open the door, flung himself toward Sophie, and then jumped straight into the business at hand.

"Sophie! Let's go on a date!"

The girl in question was in the middle of toweling off her hair. The other girls in the room shouted and screamed as they ran outside. Before long, Blade and Sophie were all alone.

"Is that an order?" she asked with her usual flat look. The only thing that was different was that, instead of wearing clothes, she was as naked as the day she was born.

"It's…not an *order*, no! But it's important! Really important!"

"All right."

"You'll do it?!"

"I'll do it."

"Woo-*hoooo*!"

Having received the okay, Blade breathed a deep sigh of relief. Now he could help Sophie enjoy the springtime of her youth—the *normal* way.

*All right! I'm gonna make this the best date ever!*

## ○ Scene V: The Shadowers

"Blade was caught peeping in the girls' changing room. We've received a large number of complaints."

"I'll hush them up."

"Also, Blade stormed into the girls' shower room. Everybody inside filed a complaint, except for one girl."

"What has gotten *into* that maniac? …I'll hush those up, too."

Earnest had a pair of opera glasses in one hand as she peered out from around the corner of a building. Claire, from the junior class, was with her. They didn't know each other all that well—but in light of current events, they had agreed to form an alliance for this covert operation.

Why? Earnest wasn't too sure, either.

"Here's some food," came a voice from above. "Take whatever you like, Empress."

A bag of bread came hurtling down toward them. Yessica—a friend of Claire's—was tagging along on their mission. Earnest tried a piece of the bread, which had come with some milk, too.

"...This is *sweet*!"

"It's meant to be. It's a dessert. Haven't you had any before?"

"Uh, um...ummm, of course!"

*I had no idea bread could be so sweet! It's delicious! Like a piece of candy!!*

Earnest washed down the candy-like treat with some milk as she gazed through her opera glasses. One block over, she found Blade, standing with his hands behind his head.

"Current time?" Earnest asked. The three of them had it on good authority that Blade's meetup time was ten in the morning.

"Ummm...I'm not exactly sure, Empress," said Claire.

*Oh. Right. Pocket watches are luxury items for most people.*

Earnest took out hers. It was a mechanical device, not magical, made with exacting precision. She opened it and read the time.

"Five more minutes."

She then handed the watch to Claire. She and Yessica stared at it curiously.

*I'm a noble, so of course I have one, but...maybe that's not so normal. Actually, why am I so preoccupied with being normal all of a sudden? This is all his* fault.

*He* was waiting for his date on the other side of her opera glasses, wearing the dopiest look she had ever seen.

"But Empress, can't we just read the time from up there?"

"Up there?"

At Yessica's observation, Earnest pointed her opera glasses upward. A large clock tower loomed right above Blade. He was standing in the main square next to the tower.

"……"

"I know Claire's a little airheaded, but does this mean you are, too, Empress?"

"Hey! That's rude!" said Claire.

"It just…wasn't in my line of s-s-sight, that's all!"

"I guess you were just paying a *lot* of attention to Blade, huh?"

"I—I—I *have* to watch him, you know!"

"Well, we have three more minutes. How's the target looking, Empress? Nervous? Excited? Freaked out? Raring to go?"

"Aren't those all pretty similar, Yessica?"

"Those are the four categories of boys as I see it."

"Which is it, Empress?" Claire asked, sounding perfectly serious.

"He's…completely normal," replied Earnest, keeping her eyes glued to him. "If I slashed at him from behind right now, I'm sure he'd dodge it."

"That's Blade for you, huh? You can't categorize him. By the way, any boy that falls into one of the four categories from before is the type you need to avoid at all costs."

"Wow, isn't that great, Empress?!"

Claire was seeking Earnest's agreement. Exactly what she thought was great wasn't clear to Earnest. She had no experience chatting with other girls, after all.

"By the way, Claire…can you stop with the 'Empress' stuff, please?"

"Oh… Okay, Lady Earnest."

"Stop *that*, too."

"Then… 'Flame Empress,' maybe?"

"That's the same as before."

"Then what *should* I call you?"

"Earnest is fine."

"Oh, no, but… That's far too informal…"

Earnest took her eyes away from her opera glasses long enough to smile at Claire. "Look, we're both here to teach that boy a lesson, aren't we? That makes us teammates. Teammates…and f-friends, I guess. Right?"

"Y-yes, certainly… Oh, but I'm not looking to beat him up or anything… I was just sort of curious, is all…"

"You liar," said Yessica. "Hee-hee… Let me tell you about this girl. Ever since Blade left our class, she's been agonizing over him every night. She stays up late, unable to sleep…"

"Whoa! I told you that was a secret!"

"Empress—sorry, Earnest—you're getting along well with Blade, and that has Claire here really worried."

"Huh? Getting along…? Well, maybe… We're friends, but…but all you have to do is remember his name and he considers you a friend, right? That's how birdbrained he is."

"That *does* sound like Blade," said Yessica.

"I swear, I have no idea what's going on with him," Earnest huffed. "Asking Sophie on a date out of nowhere…"

Earnest resisted the urge to bite her nails. That was one of the many habits she'd done away with after becoming Asmodeus's possessor at age six. Plus, she had done up her nails very nicely; she couldn't start gnawing at them.

"I'm sure Blade's, you know…," Claire began. "The Ice Queen—Sophie, I mean—she doesn't know what a 'normal' teenage life is like, right? And he feels a little responsible, and like he ought to do something about it."

"Why would he feel responsible?" asked Earnest.

"I don't know…"

The three of them looked at each other.

Blade was simply too strange, too different. It was impossible to understand what he was thinking. And so, the three girls continued to observe.

## ○ Scene VI: The Date Begins

The hand on the clock overhead moved, the gears meshing together with a *click*. The bells began to ring, signifying ten o'clock—and as the first chime sounded, Blade could already hear footsteps close by.

He looked toward the sound to find Sophie standing there. He had totally failed to notice her presence. He whistled in appreciation.

"What?"

"Nothing, I'm just really impressed."

Sophie tilted her head. She then looked over her own outfit, from her feet to her cape. She was dressed the same as always. She pulled in her scarf, checking it all the way to its far edge, then returned her gaze to Blade.

"Nothing's changed," she said.

"No, that's not what I meant…"

Trying to explain it likely wouldn't help. Blade knew several people with the natural ability to conceal their presence. It was like instinct for them—they weren't consciously aware of it. For them, it was no big deal.

"All right," he began. "Let's confirm our plan for the day. We meet here at ten hundred hours. Ten-oh-one, greetings and confirmation of the schedule. Ten-oh-three, begin traveling. Walk around the city area until ten thirty, then rest at the Parlor until eleven hundred hours. Lunch at twelve hundred. I will relay the rest of the plan at that time."

"I'll leave everything to you, since I know nothing about this kind of activity."

"You got it! I have it all worked out! I did a lot of research! Like, a *ton*!"

"Oh." Sophie lifted her head up and looked at the clock tower. "It's already ten-oh-four."

"Ahhh! Oh, crap, our plans! Our plans!!" Blade started panicking right away.

"I think we should begin traveling immediately."

Sophie took Blade's arm, and they began walking.

*Oh! Right! Our plans may have gone awry, but we're only off by one minute! Way to recover, Sophie!*

He was starting to think that they made a pretty good team.

\*

Meanwhile, back with Earnest, Claire, and Yessica—

"Ooooooh! They're walking off arm in arm! That…that's so improper!"

"Calm down, Anna. Holding each other's arm like that is perfectly normal."

"…?! 'Anna'?!" Earnest looked at Yessica like she had just insulted her.

"We're friends," Yessica replied, "so I've given you a nickname. Would you prefer Anne? or Annie, or Earn? Any suggestions?"

"Anna… Anna is fine."

The trio continued their pursuit, prudently hiding behind buildings and staying about a block behind their targets.

Blade and Sophie were walking along the waterside, traversing a long bridge that seemed to extend forever. The lake beneath them was a sparkling shade of blue.

The capital's streets and buildings were built in a series of concentric circles that fanned out from the palace in the center. The palace itself floated atop the lake, connected to the city by a series of bridges and small islands. Even in the modern era, when aerial invasions were possible, this setup offered a number of defensive advantages.

Four small islands were located around the palace, each one devoted wholly to a core section of government—politics, justice, public order, and education. The school Blade and the others attended was located on the "education" island.

The city spread in a circle around the lake; to reach the city block on the opposite bank, crossing one of the bridges was the fastest route. To cross, however, you needed the kind of security clearance students like Blade enjoyed. But that wasn't a problem for them.

The Parlor they were due to reach at ten thirty was on the other side of town. They could have just met over there to start with, but that was thinking like an amateur. They were on a *date* today, and a date…well, Blade was still a little fuzzy on the concept, despite his research, but he was pretty sure about one thing: A date was a chance for a man and a woman to enjoy idle time together.

For example, the woman needed to arrive at least half an hour after the agreed-upon meeting time. She then had to begin by saying "Sorry, did you wait long?" and then man would respond with "No, I just got here." It was like a call-and-response performance, and he wasn't sure why it was required, but it was, and that was that.

Sophie had gotten this wrong right from the start—but knowing how serious she was about everything, Blade had assumed she'd arrive exactly on time and already factored that in. This intricate plan—something Blade had spent three sleepless nights working out—couldn't be shaken by anything.

"Blade?" said Sophie.

"Hmm? What's up?"

With their arms joined like this, Sophie felt very close—her face in particular. Losing the freedom of his left arm, too, was a little…well, constricting. What if something happened? Then again, Sophie had given up use of her *right* arm.

"At this movement speed, we will not reach our destination by ten thirty," she said.

"Oh no!" *Wh-wh-what'll we do? I didn't factor our walking speed into my calculations!* Blade panicked again.

"I think we'll be fine if we walk a little faster."

"Oh! Right!"

Sophie's swift thinking instantly calmed his mind again. Blade was increasingly sure of it: They were a killer pair.

*

"...? Did they notice us?" Earnest raised an eyebrow.

Blade and Sophie were suddenly walking much faster. The trio had been careful to keep a safe distance, but maybe it hadn't been enough.

"I gotta say," Yessica commented, "Blade's date plan is gonna be pretty much impossible to carry out. It'll take a lot more than thirty minutes to cut through the palace and reach the other side. Doesn't he know that?"

"Why do you know their schedule?"

"Oh, everybody does. He was wandering around the hallways reciting it to himself."

Yessica was breezily walking in the sun, arms clasped behind her head. She was treating this more as a summer stroll than a tailing mission.

"C'mon, Claire, let's go!" she said.

"Oh, wait. I wanna give the rest of this bread to the pigeons."

Claire, meanwhile, had a flock of birds surrounding her. Earnest was a bit jealous. Small animals generally shied away from her.

"Hello, I have a reservation."

When the pair reached the Parlor, Blade placed a hand on the counter, leaned forward, and introduced himself to the lone employee.

This was a trendy place Blade had come across in his research. The entire business was located inside a large horse carriage, with tables and chairs laid out on the street for a fun open-air experience. Their menu was popular, featuring a wide variety of fruit prepared in lavish fashion; it tasted great, and it was budget-friendly, too. Many young women called it a "hidden gem" and gave it a full four stars.

"Pardon?" The Parlor employee shot Blade a funny look. Maybe he hadn't heard him.

"I said I had a reservation—"

"Oh, right. Take any seat you like."

"Thank you."

Blade tried to find the sunniest table, then reconsidered and went for one located under an umbrella. He changed his mind after recalling how Sophie preferred to stand in the shade most days. Her skin was pale, so she probably wasn't very partial to intense sunlight. He was so considerate, he was making himself dizzy with pride.

"So, um. There's no waitstaff here. You just order and pay at the counter, all right?"

"Sure thing," Blade replied. He knew all that, of course. This establishment provided a mind-blowing service—one of the secrets behind its immense popularity. It was called "self-service," and it was very hard to find anywhere else.

"What should we get to drink?" Sophie asked from her spot in the shade.

"Wait! Don't rush it!"

Blade raised a hand to stop her. An amateur might have picked something at random from the menu just now. But Blade was no amateur. He knew about the *special drink* you just had to order when on a date.

"We'll have one Lovely Infinite Tropical, please."

He approached the carriage, putting one large-value bill on the counter.

"Oh, sure thing. One Love Juice, coming right up."

What an abbreviation! It wasn't a very good abbreviation, either. Now Blade was concerned his order hadn't been understood.

"Oh, sir, your change…"

"You can keep it."

"I—I can't take this much, sir…"

The employee shoved a small dragon's hoard of coins toward Blade, making him feel extraordinarily uncool. This, too, made him dizzy, but he fought off the sensation as he brought the juice back to Sophie.

"This drink is served inside an entire fruit from the southern lands," he explained. "You drink it via this two-way straw. Our mission here is to finish it."

"Oh. So just drink this?"

"Wait!" Blade suddenly explained. "It's still ten twenty-nine. We're a minute too early! I think we hurried a bit too much earlier."

"I'm thirsty," said Sophie.

"Y-you are? Well…it won't hurt, I guess…"

He pointed one end of the two-way straw toward Sophie, bringing his lips to the other. This was a co-op mission. If they didn't suck on the straw together, the juice wouldn't rise.

"Mmph!"

But *man*, was her face close to his. Her beautiful features were so near, his eyes couldn't focus on them.

"This is hard to drink," she said. "Come closer."

*Slap.* Now their cheeks were touching.

"Ahhh! Ahhh! Ahhh!" Blade leaned away, putting some distance back between them.

"What's wrong?"

"It's like… I dunno, like… Just now, like…"

An unfamiliar feeling had coursed through Blade's body the moment their cheeks brushed together.

"Like what? …What's wrong?"

"N-no… It's nothing. Let's resume the mission. Sorry."

"Oh."

Sophie waited, her end of the straw in her mouth. Unbelievably, she had her eyes closed. Blade tensed up.

*I…I can't! This is…like, extremely impossible! Going over there to get that cheek-on-cheek action again… I can't!!*

"It is impossible for me to complete this mission by myself," Sophie said, blinking. "I require your assistance."

There was no way Blade could let her down.

"I…I know… I know, but… One second. My heart…"

Blade caught his breath. Long ago, a martial-arts master who lived in a shack atop a high mountain had taught him a breathing technique that let him take in the air and the earth and make their power his own.

*Sky above, earth below, mankind in between...lend me your strength! Your courage!! The courage to let my cheek brush hers!!*

As a Hero, Blade had never once prayed before battle. But now, for the first time in his life, he did just that.

Earnest and the others had pretty much given up on stealth. Blade and Sophie had showed no signs of noticing them, and they'd grown increasingly bold. The three of them were currently at the exact same juice place, drinking from the exact same menu, watching the pair from the table farthest away.

"It's actually going pretty normally, isn't it?" said Claire.

"Yeah," agreed Yessica. "Maybe we didn't need to worry."

"All they're doing is drinking juice, after all."

"It's delicious, too. Come on, help me out. This really *is* a two-person job."

"Oh. Okay, Yessica."

Claire and Yessica were seated next to each other, their cheeks practically glued together as they cheerfully slurped away at the two-way straw.

"Disgusting! Filthy! Unsanitary! Monstrous! Y-y-your cheeks are touching! Y-your cheeks! Your *cheeks*!"

"Here, Anna, you should try this. It's good."

Yessica pointed to an item on the menu—not a juice to drink, but some frozen milk you ate with a spoon. A few minutes later, Earnest was gushing.

"Wowww! It's sweet! How can it be so sweet?!" The moment she put some in her mouth, the sheer tastiness shocked her. "And *collld!* But so good!!"

Soon, Earnest was in her own little world, just her and the icy treat.

"It's called a 'parfait.'"

Yessica was saying something, but Earnest couldn't hear her. She was too busy cursing the tiny spoon that had come with her order. Couldn't they have given her a bigger one?!

"Oh, right!" said Claire. "Hey, Yessica, I think an opera I wanted to see is starting later."

"Mmm, I'd prefer a concert myself. What about you, Anna? Anyplace you wanna go?"

"Huh? Don't be silly! We're on a mission, aren't we?!" Earnest's face shot up from the parfait as she shouted. The other two had completely forgotten why they were here. Totally incompetent!

"But they're already gone. Um, what were they doing starting at noon, again?"

"Eating lunch, right?"

"What?" Earnest froze as Claire dabbed her mouth with a napkin. She looked over—and Blade was gone.

*No! I was so distracted by the parfait, I let them out of my sight…! I… Earnest Flaming…have never been so humiliated!*

"Oh, did we lose them? Ah, well."

Blade looked back, sensing that their pursuers had disappeared at some point.

He had noticed them, of course—right away, in fact. It was rare for him *not* to be pursued, for fair reasons or foul, so he didn't even pay attention to it most of the time. He had only registered the current group's presence once they were gone. Were they spies for the king? Or from some other country? Whatever. He was a normal person now, so it didn't matter to him.

Blade looked at Sophie and asked if she could sense anything. Sophie's well-formed chin swung left and right as she shook her head; she also believed their pursuers had left. His gut told him that she was better at this stuff than he was, so if she couldn't detect anything, he figured they were really gone.

"Well, moving on." He crossed his arms behind his head. It was time for the next item on the schedule. "Oh crap!"

That was when he noticed. Their next activity was a meal at 1200 hours…at a restaurant clear across the capital.

*Noooo! I forgot to factor in transport time again!*

There was no way they could walk there in time. Even if they ran the whole way, it was physically impossible.

"N-n-n-*now* what'll we do…?" Blade looked to Sophie, his eyes scrunched up in dismay.

"It's all right," she said, as cool as ever. "Let's take a shortcut."

She reached out her arm, and Blade returned the gesture. Their fingers interlaced. Then Sophie began to run, keeping a firm grip on Blade's hand. She was tearing down the road, toward the exterior of a building.

With a quick three-step motion, she began running straight up the wall, dragging Blade along with her as she scaled the three-story brick building.

Once atop the roof, their view opened up again. From there, they could keep going straight ahead as far as they wished. Blade followed Sophie as she rushed across roofs and leaped over alleyways.

*Ah, yes. If we can't make it running normally, then why not try something a little more abnormal? Sophie… She's so smart!*

Blade was absolutely certain now—he and Sophie made the best combo in the world.

## ○ Scene VII: End of the Date

"Today was fun."

"Awww…"

Being told this point-blank made Blade a little embarrassed.

The dating manual he'd read had advised that "if she says she enjoyed it at the end, the date's a big success—and maybe it'll lead to even *bigger* things! ♡" He honestly didn't know what kind of "bigger things ♡" the author meant, but it seemed safe to call this a win.

In fact, the date had been absolutely perfect. Every item on the schedule went off without a hitch.

They'd made it to the restaurant by tearing across the city's roofs. He hadn't factored in the interminable wait for their food, but they both managed to wolf it down in five minutes and bug out. Then it was off to an art museum, and thanks to their new parkour skills, reaching the other side of the capital was no longer a chore. They played a bunch of games at an arcade after that, only to break a "test your punch" machine and find themselves obligated to head out ten minutes early. This concerned Blade a little, but Sophie made a brilliant suggestion ("I want to feed the fish"), and that consumed the ten minutes quite nicely. Blade was reminded again that they made a truly fantastic team. As they enjoyed their next activity, window shopping, Blade was certain he saw Sophie's eyes move despite her blank expression when she faced a display of young women's wear. This was window shopping, though, not *shopping* shopping, so they had to leave without purchasing anything. Then, in order to catch the best sunset possible, they went to the highest point in town—the towering spire at the very top of the palace—only to take a thrilling sprint back down in order to reach a bar five minutes later. The tavern was nice, but both of them knew that alcohol destroyed brain cells, so they opted for some juice as they looked at all the liquor bottles. All in all, a brilliant time.

Now a night breeze was blowing as they looked out at the lake. There was a little time before curfew at the dorm, but they had no more plans for the day. Blade was totally exhausted and greatly relieved.

"Can I ask a question?" Sophie said softly, her hand against her blue hair to keep the breeze from blowing it around.

Blade looked back at her. "Hmm? Sure. Ask me anything."

"Why did you do all of this for me?"

"Why…? Um…"

Blade didn't know what to say. He had wanted to teach her what the "springtime of youth" was supposed to be like. It was his duty, after all.

She had been robbed of any chance of a normal life thanks to the existence of the Hero—of Blade.

"Uhm... Well, I mean, you... You're..."

No. He couldn't say it. If he brought up Sophie's role in the Manmade Hero Project or whatever it was called, he'd have to admit to her that he was the Hero. He wasn't keeping it a secret, exactly; telling her shouldn't have bothered him. But it was no use. He just couldn't say it.

*I mean...if I said that...then Sophie would...*

She'd know that her life had been all scrambled up thanks to Blade. And if she learned that... Well, that's why he couldn't.

"Sorry. Never mind," he said.

"Oh." Sophie was curt as usual. She looked away from the lake and began to walk in the direction of the dorms.

"Because we're friends!" Blade finally shouted at her back.

"...Friends?" Sophie turned around.

"Yeah. Because we're friends. So...this much is a given. You don't have to worry about it."

"Me...and you...are friends?"

"Y-yeah. Of course we are."

"Oh." She gave a slight nod and paused for a moment, thinking. "I heard that friends don't keep secrets from each other."

*Gullllllllp!*

"W-well, um..."

"So listen to me."

"S-sure!"

Blade stood there, unable to move an inch.

"There's something I haven't told you about."

*Hmm? I thought she was going to accuse* me *of keeping secrets. But now she's saying she has one...?*

"If we're...friends... If you are willing to become my friend...then I need you to hear something."

She looked deadly serious, like she was about to make an important confession. So Blade looked back at her, just as serious. He had a pretty good idea of what she was about to say. Despite that, Blade was so overwhelmed by the atmosphere around the expressionless girl that he simply stood quietly and listened.

"I...I was born to become a manmade Hero. But I am not complete. I am an incomplete test subject." The anxiety behind this confession was clear despite her flat expression. "If I seem inhuman to you...that is likely the reason."

"Of course you're human. What're you talking about?" Blade couldn't stop himself. He had intended to keep quiet and listen, but he spoke up anyway.

"I am modeled after a super-being known as a Hero. It is only natural that I seem superhuman—"

"The *Hero's* human, too!" he said, unconsciously shouting. What was he saying? Why had he shouted it? Nothing made sense.

"......"

After a moment of silence, Sophie continued, "I...am not so sure. I have never met the Hero. All I was given was the power that makes the Hero what he is. An artificial Hero force. That is what they called it."

*Huh? What's that now?*

For a moment, Blade thought he had misheard her. He knew she had been a test subject—the king himself had said as much. She was part of a project devised to create a Hero from thin air. Sophie was one of the project's victims, and she'd likely been the subject of immeasurable abuse from a young age, forced to undergo countless horrible experiments. That explained why she was such a menace in the arena. How many grueling hours of training did it require to attain such a high level of skill at *her* age...? Blade had a feeling he knew. He had suffered through a similar childhood as the "real" Hero, an ordeal that may have lasted even longer than hers.

*But... No way. No way.*

He had never dreamed that the Manmade Hero Project had managed to artificially craft the power that made a Hero a Hero. Power like *that* wasn't the kind of thing you could just synthesize in a lab.

"Watch this," she said.

Sophie's entire body began to glow a dull blue color. Blade saw it—and then he shuddered.

*This light… This glow… It's almost like…*

The metal handrail beneath Sophie's fingers suddenly twisted, then slowly fell to the ground, like a stick of melting butter. It wasn't caused by high temperature—the material *itself* had changed. Like the metal had forgotten it was supposed to be hard.

"I have incomplete control over it." Sophie looked at the handrail as if she was surprised, then pulled back her hand. Next, she hopped in place—just a few inches into the air. But when she landed—

*Ka-boooom!*

—there was a loud roar. The sturdy stone paving of the walkway collapsed, forming a conical crater with Sophie in the middle.

"I multiplied my weight by a thousand times…or I intended to. It wound up being around ten thousand instead."

This wasn't sorcery. Sorcery *could* do this, perhaps, but Blade knew that wasn't what he was seeing. As a former Hero, he knew.

This was it. *This* was the power.

"Time stop," Sophie whispered.

Immediately, the world was repainted in shades of gray. The wind died down—or rather, it stopped cold. The leaves on the trees lining the walkway were still. So were the waves on the surface of the lake. Blade couldn't even blink.

Through this world, frozen in time, Sophie began to walk. She went to Blade, brushed a hand against his cheek, then went back. Once she returned to her original position, the dim blue glow around her went out like a light.

Now Blade could move again. He could feel the wind. The leaves rustled continuously, and the waves rolled on.

"I can even stop time. Currently, I can activate my artificial Hero force for only ten seconds."

Her face looked strained now. Even her eyes looked sunken. It had taken only ten seconds to exhaust her within an inch of her life.

"You..." Somehow, Blade moved his throat and managed to speak.

"I am Sophitia Femto. The twelfth clone of a woman named Sophitia. That is who I am: The final test subject of the Manmade Hero Project...and its sole success story, though that success was not unqualified."

"I... I..." Blade groaned.

Sophie had revealed her secret to him and told him about her cursed past. Now Blade needed to do the same. Friends didn't keep secrets from each other. She had said so herself, and Blade agreed with her.

He should tell her. No—if he wanted to be her friend, he had to!

"Listen!"

"I am listening."

"I... I—I am...the...the H..." Blade summoned all his courage. He needed more of it now than he ever had before. "...the...the H-H..."

Sophie patiently waited for him. He knew she'd wait as long as it took. And the moment he realized that, he was able to say it.

"...the Hero!"

Sophie's face froze.

"I...am the Hero," he continued. "Or I was...I guess. Now...I'm not the Hero anymore. I no longer have...that power."

"Oh." Sophie nodded, looking unaffected.

"Did you...already know that?" Blade had to ask. She seemed wholly unsurprised by the revelation. But she shook her head.

"No. I had a hunch, though. A big one. You just seemed so familiar to me, even though we'd never met before. It was strange."

"Yeah." Blade nodded listlessly.

He felt he understood what she meant. He'd felt a kindred spirit in Sophie, too. Blade, for his part, sympathized deeply with her isolation from the rest of society, though what she felt might have been a little different...

"What's wrong?" Sophie asked. The question made Blade realize he was staring at her.

"Oh... I'm just really sorry... Though I know it's not something an apology can fix. Go ahead and hate me if you like. I'd understand."

"Why would I hate you?"

"Huh?"

That was a surprising question. Who wouldn't hate him if they were in her position? Because of his existence, she'd been cursed—forced to live as a manmade Hero.

"I...I didn't become a Hero because I wanted to. But I am... I mean, I *was* the Hero..."

"Which one is it?" Sophie asked. Blade blushed.

"I—I was the Hero, but now I'm not, and ummm..."

"I'm sorry. Continue."

"But I...yeah. I didn't want to be the Hero. But I had no choice. I mean, I can *save* people. Or I could. So it wasn't like I could say no... I *had* to do it, right?"

He looked at Sophie. She nodded, giving him the drive to keep going.

"But having the power of a Hero doesn't mean you can save everyone and everything. Sometimes, you *can't* save people. Or even whole towns. I tried to help everyone out...but sometimes I lost people dear to me in the process..."

He swallowed the rest of his words. Painful memories passed through his mind, preventing him from doing anything for a few seconds.

"But when I can't help people...they all get mad at me. Like, 'Why couldn't you save us? Why? You're the *Hero!*'"

Visions of the past came flooding back. Usually, he tried to forget about things like this. He *had* forgotten.

Blade's Hero power had manifested at the age of three. He didn't know his parents, or even his real name. A mercenary boss later told him that he was named Blade because as a little kid, he had held on to a sword for dear life in the middle of a battlefield.

Once his power manifested, he was trained by the greatest champions of his nation—of the whole continent. That was the only reason why Blade still had access to so many otherworldly, powerful skills. If another person was raised in the same environment with the same experiences, they would've become just as powerful.

But Blade didn't want anyone else to follow in his footsteps. Nobody should have to go through the things he had. He had walked the line between life and death many times. He had considered taking the easy way out and simply letting himself die more than once. But he got back up every time, never crossing that line. If the Hero fell, someone else in the world would inherit the Hero's power. That was how the world worked. The Hero and the Overlord were evenly matched. If the Hero fell without defeating the Overlord, someone else would have to take the Hero's path instead. That accursed path.

"I... I..." Blade was clinging to Sophie. She reached out to caress his hair. "What...what even *is* a Hero?"

She didn't answer. She just kept stroking his head.

Blade already understood, however. A Hero's power was a type of curse. Once afflicted, you were forced into this gigantic, preordained destiny, as the biggest cog in the whole machine.

"Whether you wanted to become one or not, you were still a Hero."

Blade listened to Sophie speak as she caressed him. He was getting her stomach all wet with tears, but he gritted his teeth and endured, refusing to sob out loud.

"Before I could be disposed of, the king rescued me from the facility where I was being held. I didn't know what I was, so I went on a journey. This was before I entered school. I met so many people and visited so many towns that the Hero had saved."

She kept quietly caressing him as she spoke. It felt so comfortable.

"You've given courage to a great many people. Whenever someone says the word 'Hero,' it plants the light of hope in their hearts. All the anguish you went through... It didn't go to waste."

Blade clung to Sophie's stomach. Somehow, that reassured him. Maybe this was how it felt to be held close by a mother. He wouldn't know.

"You should be proud of that," she said at last.

"I can't," he replied. Somehow, he felt safe complaining about his fate to Sophie.

"That's fine."

She forgave him. That had never happened before. Everyone, to a man, always said, "You're the Hero, so keep trying for us." But Sophie had finally given him permission to just exist. He didn't *have* to keep doing his best.

"But I'm proud of being born a manmade Hero," she said.

Blade stopped clinging to her. He was reluctant to let go, but he had shed enough tears. Lifting up his head, he gazed at Sophie. He wasn't hugging her anymore. He stood up tall, matched her height, and looked her straight in the eye.

"I—"

"I'm aiming to be someone like you," she said, eyes boring into him. She had placed her full trust in him.

Blade wiped his eyes with his sleeve. "I bet you hate it when a man cries, don't you?"

"I don't mind."

"Well, I...um, I..."

"Go ahead."

"I—! I won't be troubled...by my past as a Hero anymore."

"Fine. If that's what you've decided."

Sophie smiled. It was the tiniest of smiles, barely perceptible, but Blade was certain that's what it was. Her face was illuminated by the pair of moons that always shone at the same place in the night sky—one big, one small.

"Your Hero past will be our secret," she said, her smile practically glittering.

"Yeah. Of course."

Blade nodded firmly. He wiped his hands on his pants, then exchanged a stiff handshake with Sophie.

Just then, something urgent occurred to him.

"Ah! Oh crap, our curfew!"

"Even if we ran at full speed, we would have less than a one percent chance of arriving on time."

Blade laughed. "It's a Hero's job to make the impossible possible, right? And we have almost a one percent chance! Bring it on."

They grabbed each other's hands and ran for the school.

## Chapter 3:
# Cú Chulainn

○ **Scene I: Lunch as Usual**

It was lunch as usual. The now-familiar table, pretty much reserved seating at this point, was full of people.

"Veggies only for lunch again, Claire?" said Earnest. "You need to eat more, or you won't make it through the drills this afternoon."

"Um, I'm kind of on a diet... I tend to gain weight easily, so..."

"No, no, no," protested Leonard. "You're pretty exactly as you are! I think you're at just the right weight for a girl... Right, Blade? You agree, don't you?"

"*Mmmmmm!* I love this katsu curry so much!"

"Leonard...," said Earnest. "Not that I mind, but why are you here?"

"Well, with so many charming girls gathered in one place, how could I *not* be here?"

"Hey, Anna, can you introduce me to this hottie?" said Yessica. "I just *love* a shallow man!"

"Mmm? Anna? Who's that?"

"Oh, just eat your curry, Blade... C'mon, Anna, help a girl out!"

"Will you knock that off already, Yessica? What happens if Blade starts calling me that, too?"

"Calling you what?"

"Just shut up and eat, already!"

"*Mmmmmm!* I love this katsu curry so *much*!!"

"Ah... Hang on, Blade, you have curry on your face...!"

"I'll wipe it, since I'm next to him. Here, Blade."

"Mmm? What's up, Sophie?"

"Oh, okay then..."

"Why hello there, lovely lady. You're quite the charmer. There's something so *wild* about you."

"Ah-ha-ha-ha-ha! I love it! This guy's the best! You wanna be my man? I'm ready for you anytime!"

"Oh... My apologies. I simply can't allow myself to be tied down. I love every woman in the universe."

"*Bah*-ha-ha-ha-ha-ha-ha-ha-ha-ha!"

This used to be Earnest's table. There was seating for eight, but for some reason, she'd had it all to herself. Then Blade had helped himself to a seat, and with Blade there, Sophie joined as well; and then Claire and Yessica appeared, calling themselves friends of Earnest...and now it was as boisterous as any other lunch table. As for Leonard, well, Blade didn't really care why he was there, but he had a sneaking suspicion that Leonard had been telling the truth earlier.

"Phew, I'm full..." Blade patted his stomach appreciatively.

He'd had to keep his meals light during his Hero days, since stuffing himself wasn't conducive to the quick moves needed in combat; only recently had he been able to enjoy food like this. Being normal was *so* awesome.

"You eat that every day, don't you?"

Earnest had been chatting with Claire and Yessica only a moment ago, but her keen senses caught Blade just in time to start berating him. She was referring to the katsu curry that he incessantly ate for lunch.

"No, it's only about every other day. The spice, you know... It's *so* addictive. And the meat, too! Whoever thought to cover it in bread crumbs and fry it up like that? They've gotta be a super genius."

"That spicy sauce is from the south. The *katsu* cutlets were invented in this kingdom, though."

"Wow, Earnest, you know a lot."

"Wait... That's c-common knowledge, right...? Everyone knows that."

Earnest always reacted to compliments with intense shame. It was kind of weird. All that aside, things had really gotten livelier around the former Empress. When Blade first became her friend, she was practically radiating loner vibes—but now people naturally gathered around her.

"Hey, y'know, you haven't done that thing to me lately," said Blade.

"What thing?" Earnest replied.

"You know. Your killer glare."

"Huh? What do you mean?"

Looks of recognition spread across the table, though Earnest herself seemed puzzled. Everyone took Blade's side. Only Earnest seemed out of the loop, though Sophie—currently chomping on some fruit next to Blade—was a little hard to read.

"Oh, right!" Earnest said, trying to redirect the conversation. "I hope all of you saved some space, because I have a special dessert for us today."

Taking everyone's smiles as evidence of their agreement, she called out to a woman behind the dining hall counter.

"Madam, if you could!"

The lunch lady, who always gave Blade big helpings, heeded Earnest's signal and brought in a large cake—even bigger than her ample bosom. She then placed it at the center of the table.

Earnest looked at Claire and Yessica. "Congratulations, you two. You're both officially in the senior class. Make sure to tell Clayde and Kassim later, too, all right? His Majesty the Chancellor should send both of you official notices as soon as he beats back all the paperwork on his desk."

"Ahhhh!"

"Wowww!"

Shrieks of delight filled the dining hall. Experiencing them at point-blank range hurt their friends' eardrums a little.

"This is my gift to you, all right? Eat up."

Even Earnest, once feared as the Empress, was capable of change. She'd started a tradition of holding celebrations for students promoted to the senior class.

"Huh? U-um... I-I'm not sure I should be having this much dessert right now..." Claire raised an eyebrow at the gigantic cake set before her.

"Oh? You don't like cake?"

"No, I love it... I *really* love it, but... *Nnnngh*..."

"Well, perfect. This cake is really good, too, you know. *Very* sweet. I can hardly believe such delicacies exist in this world! I feel like I've been wasting my life!"

"I'm sorry, Anna... You can have my portion... Ohhh, no, no, I can't stop myself! I'll have a piece! Whatever! I don't care!" Claire took the largest slice.

"By the way, Blade, did you hear the news?" Earnest had a bit of cream on the edge of her mouth as she spoke.

"What news?" Blade replied, his lips just as messy. He let Sophie wipe them for him.

"There's talk of a magic beast being sent to the school."

"A magic beast?"

"Yeah. I guess...*homph*...His Majesty was keen on having us...*chomp*...get some more realistic training, so...*homph, homph*..."

"Can you please decide if you're going to eat or talk?"

"......"

"Don't choose eating!"

"...Like I was saying, I heard that we're going to receive a magic beast so we can get more experience with that kind of combat. Apparently, His Majesty's working to secure a really strong one—not the kind we normally see."

"Hmm."

"'Hmm'? What do you mean, 'hmm'? We're talking about a *magic beast*."

You could find such beasts anytime you wanted on the frontier. Camp out in the wastes, and you could expect to be attacked every other night, on average. Having to wake up all the time to deal with them tended to result in a terrible night's sleep, so you needed to learn how to attack without waking up—cutting them in half while you were still snoozing—or else you'd be exhausted come morning...

It was around this point that Blade realized his line of thought was probably not normal.

"Wow, really?" he said. "That's neat. Kinda scary, too."

"...You're a terrible liar, you know."

"Well... This is just what I'd expect from that dude... He has such poor taste."

"'That dude'? Come on, Blade, aren't you being a little rude to His Majesty?"

"Oh, it's fine. 'That dude' suits him way better than 'His Majesty.'"

Blade had to admit the king wasn't totally off base. You could train against human opponents forever, but that would only prepare you to fight humans—and looking back at his life as a Hero, far more of his opponents had been of the nonhuman variety.

No wonder they called the king the Lion Monarch—the tyrant could probably best most champions in a fight. It made sense he would be practical.

...It was still in poor taste, though.

## ○ Scene II: It

Its hunger was intense.

It was locked into a cramped space, being taken to parts unknown. To be exact, it was in a metal cage equipped with a magic-powered barrier. Parts of its body touched the barrier whenever there was a bump on the road, causing sparks to fly. Each time, it suffered pain and agony.

Chains crafted from divine metal coiled around its body—impossible to break with sheer force alone. Normally, it could breathe fire to blow the barrier away...but with the muzzle affixed to its mouth, that wasn't an option.

It had enjoyed a leisurely life, setting up its stronghold deep inside a labyrinth, until it was attacked and captured by these weak, conniving creatures. In a fair fight, there was no way it would have lost, no matter how many opponents it faced. Its strength was simply too far beyond their meager capabilities. But these little creatures, cowards that they were, set a trap for it.

And so it was caught and taken away, its freedom stolen, its pride wounded. The fact that the little creatures didn't immediately kill and eat it was yet another humiliation.

The scent of tasty-smelling meat wafted in from somewhere. Its stomach growled, much to its annoyance. It was intensely hungry. Raw meat was regularly dropped into its cage, but its instincts demanded it eat nothing it had not hunted itself or received from its parent.

"Hey, it's time to eat! You're gonna die if you don't!"

A small creature appeared in front of its cage. A frail one, so much tinier than *it*. No fangs, no claws, not even any poison.

"...Oh, you can't eat with that on, can you? Let's take that off."

The muzzle was removed. This small, stupid creature had finally done it.

With its free mouth, it exhibited a vicious smile.

*You small, crafty creatures... It is time you faced my wrath.*

## ○ Scene III: Dragon

"Huh?" Blade strained his ears, sensing something nearby.

"What's up?" Earnest asked. She looked at Sophie to his side. She, too, had pricked up her ears, focused on some point ahead of them.

"Guys, what are you doing?" Earnest asked, before gasping and turning toward the corridor leading out of the dining hall.

"What're you three doing?" asked Yessica with a smile.

Then she saw Leonard, too, had his well-honed face pointed straight at the exit. The sight silenced her.

"Oh, am I next?" asked Claire. "Is it my turn now? Hey, what's up with the five of you?"

"I think we should probably evacuate the dining hall, Earnest."

"I agree. Lend me a hand, Sophie."

The girls in red and blue stood up together, then split up. Yessica and Leonard each followed one of them.

"Huh? What? What's going on?"

Claire was left looking around helplessly, accompanied only by Blade, who was still chowing down on his katsu curry. He had picked up another helping after he finished his slice of cake, so this was actually round three for him.

"Attention!"

Earnest's voice rang out. The dining hall instantly fell silent. She still knew how to play the Empress, it seemed.

"Follow our instructions and evacuate immediately! No talking, no questions! Now! Hurry up!"

"Ugh... Really?" Blade stood up, whining to himself. Taking his plate of curry with him, he headed toward the corridor.

Before he could finish eating, Blade reached the site of the incident. He looked between *it* and his plate, wondering what to do.

Several instructors had their weapons out and pointed at the thing. Only two of them had any armor on, and even then, it was just a helmet on one and a single gauntlet on the other. Nobody was equipped for battle—didn't they realize they were as good as dead if they went to the front line like that? If you can't put on your armor in thirty seconds, you better sleep in it. Eesh.

"Hey! Look out! Get back!"

One of the instructors turned around and yelled at him. Wasn't *he* the one in more danger here? He had his lance out and pointed at *it*, but he was weak in the knees and looked ready to run at a moment's notice. Their target took a step forward, and the instructors all took a step back. They weren't even keeping it at bay.

Wherever this adversary escaped from, it must have destroyed well near everything it caught sight of. The path it had taken to get here was obvious. The main hall of the school building was quite wide, almost needlessly so, but it was still a bit too narrow for *it*. Anytime one of its shoulders or wings brushed against one of the wooden walls or columns, splinters went flying. Stone walls would warp outward and shudder as the blocks were knocked loose.

"*Fwrrsshh...*"

It stopped moving and exhaled deeply, as if to intimidate Blade. Its flaming breath might be a threat, but using it would require it to open its mouth wide and suck in a large breath—and that took time. In fact, it took about as long as it did to charge up Dragon Eater. Earnest had pointed out to him in the past that Dragon Eater wasn't a very practical move, and she was absolutely right. Dragons' breath was a threat only when you were dealing with a whole pack of them at once. Up against just one, it was easy to avoid.

*Hmm? So this one's smart, huh.*

Blade had expected a bolt of flame breath just now. He had repositioned himself to prepare for it, ensuring that nothing but hallway, walls, and the lake were behind him. But this dragon must've understood it wouldn't be effective, because it didn't try to attack with its breath. Considering it was still immature, it seemed pretty intelligent.

"C-call for the king!" one of the instructors shouted. "He's the only one who can handle a dragon..."

The others nodded, appreciating this suggestion, and they all retreated at top speed. *This kingdom is doomed.* Instead of defending their king, the soldiers were asking their king to defend *them*! Why didn't anyone shout "We'll serve as shields while the king retreats!" *Of course, that lout's so strong that there's no need to defend him...*

...Right. Now what? Blade thought for a moment, the curry plate still in his hand. He was sure that bum of a king had received a report of the escaped dragon and just said, *It's fine,* he'll *take care of it* without even lifting his eyes from his paperwork. Blade had been eating lunch like a normal person, so naturally he was unarmed. Normal people didn't come to lunch with a weapon. Only someone like Earnest would keep a sword on her at all times.

"Blade! I'll join you!" came a voice from the other end of the hallway.

Well. Speak of the devil. Earnest had probably run back after making sure the other students had evacuated, and she wasn't alone. Several students ready to defend the school were with her, all bearing weapons.

*Better hurry.*

Blade took a step forward. He would have liked a wooden sword, or at least a mop…but oh well. *This* works, too.

He raised an arm up high, spinning it hard from the shoulder.

*"Fffsh!"*

The dragon breathed at him. Hot embers danced in the air. Dragons' metabolism went into overdrive when they entered battle mode, bringing the temperature of their breath to the ignition point.

Blade hurled the curry plate in his hand into the air. Then, with a light hop, he put all his weight into his right fist, and—

"Sit."

—plunged it down from above into the dragon's upper jaw. The dragon's mouth was open, ready to bite, but it snapped shut as its ponderous head smashed to the ground. Bits of stone flew into the air as the impact formed a crater several feet deep.

"Right."

Its new position was probably more "lie down" than "sit," but either way, the dragon wouldn't be causing any harm now.

The plate Blade had thrown earlier was coming down fast. He caught it with his free hand. The rice hit the ceramic dish first, the curry following close behind, and finally the cutlet slices landed on top, reconstituting the katsu curry.

"Ah..."

He didn't quite catch the pickles in time, however.

"Awww..."

He crouched, looking at them on the ground. As he wondered whether the five-second rule still applied in this situation—

"B-Blade... Wait, what...? What are you *doing?*"

—Earnest called out to him frantically.

"Uh, the pickles..."

"Not *that*! I mean, just now...!"

"Oh, this little guy? Yeah, it should be fine for now."

Blade reached out and petted the baby dragon's head. It growled a little. He knew from experience that once you whipped a dragon's ass, it tended to calm down.

"It's still a baby... You were just scared, weren't you?" he cooed.

*Growwwl.*

"A baby? But it's still a dragon, isn't it...?"

"You hungry, kid?" The baby dragon seemed interested in the katsu curry in Blade's hand. "Want this?" He brought the food up to its snout—

—and its large tongue lapped the whole thing up, plate and all.

"Guess you did, huh?"

Then a plume of fire erupted from the dragon's mouth.

"Ha-ha! Too spicy for ya?" Blade smiled just as people began to gather around him. The scene quickly grew raucous, and before long, it dawned on him that he was the center of attention.

"Hey... Just now... He did him in...barehanded, didn't he?"

He could hear the rubberneckers commenting on him.

"Well, I mean, I didn't see any weapons lying around!" said Blade. *I knew barehanded was a bad idea. That's why I wanted a mop.* "See? It hurt, too!"

He showed off his hand. The skin was peeling around the knuckles. There was even some bleeding.

*There! You see? Look at this! It's not like I can punch a dragon and emerge unscathed!*

A dragon's scales hardened on impact, so melee combat was the worst way to take one down.

"I've never heard of anything like it... A dragon, in one blow..."

*Huh? That's what they found so impressive?!*

"Come on! That's totally normal! Besides, this one's still just a baby! It's not a Great Dragon, and it's *certainly* no Ancient Dragon."

Great Dragons were a force to be reckoned with, to say nothing of an Ancient Dragon with over a thousand years under its belt. But *this*? This was just a kid.

"Anyone could take this guy out in one shot! I mean it!"

Blade desperately tried to defend himself. He wasn't lying or talking nonsense, either. Among the people Blade knew, most could do what he'd just done. Though come to think of it, the number that couldn't was steadily rising as of late, particularly among the friends he had made at school.

*Um? Uhhh...? I'm normal, right? This is definitely normal. I sure hope it is anyway...*

He looked at the others.

"Like, I mean... I'm not, um... H-hey, stop looking at me like that...!"

*Don't look at me! Not like that—like I'm some kind of super-being!*

"Ugh! You idiot!" A red figure emerged from the crowd and slapped Blade on the cheek. "Look at how much destruction you caused! You could have *tried* to keep the damage to a minimum, at least!"

"Y-yeah, but I took it down in one hit," Blade said, rubbing his cheek.

"You didn't have to destroy the floor in the process! You're lucky we're on the ground level! If we were upstairs, there'd be a gaping hole in the floor!"

Blade looked back at the raging Earnest.

*I think she just gave me a nosebleed...*

The hand he'd used to punch the dragon suddenly felt oddly warm... like it was enveloped in something.

The dragon was licking his hand, bloody knuckles and all. It wasn't trying to eat him—it was almost like it was trying to help with his wounds.

"Blade... Blade!" Claire ran up to him and pulled his hand out of the dragon's mouth, holding it in her hands despite the saliva that was now getting all over her. A strange glow covered his fist, and then, before his very eyes, the cuts on his hand healed.

*Healing magic? ...No. Restoration, maybe?*

"I'm still not very good, but this is what qualified me for the senior class... I'll help you out whenever you need me, okay?"

Claire had fixed his hand. She fixed his nosebleed, too, while she was at it.

"All right, people, don't just stand there like fools!" Earnest said, clapping her hands. "Someone call His Majesty over! If you're free, help clear out the rubble! You! You instructors standing around over there! I expect you to help, too!"

She was ordering everyone around, students and teachers alike, but Blade was grateful to her. She might have slapped him silly, but it had helped distract everyone and allowed him to escape a sticky situation.

"Blade, you too... Huh?"

When he looked at Earnest, she was staring back at him. They locked eyes, and Blade waved his hand as an expression of thanks. But Earnest stayed frozen.

*Huh?* Blade looked around at everyone else. They were all gawping at him in abject shock.

*What did I do this time?*

Claire, still gripping his arm, was looking at something over Blade's shoulder, her mouth agape. Only Sophie remained unaffected, no expression on her face as she pointed to a spot behind him.

*Behind me?* Blade turned around.

"Honored Father!"

Or rather, he *tried* to turn around. But just then, a little kid ran up and hugged him around his neck. When he finally managed to look behind him, he found...nothing. The dragon—that gigantic creature—had vanished without a trace.

And in its place, a little girl was hanging from his neck. He spun around, but she refused to let go, gripping him tight.

"Who's *this*?"

"So you were my parent! I've been searching for so long! I had such a hard time without you. All these little creatures ganged up on me—it was *so* annoying! But I'm very tolerant, so I'm willing to put all that behind me depending on your reaction. So you have to give me *lots* of attention! Lots!"

"What're you talking about? Why is a kid like you here? Where are your parents?"

"Right here!"

This was going nowhere. Blade turned to Earnest, the child still clinging to his back.

"Where did it go?" he asked. "Where's the baby dragon?"

"It—it—it… Th-th-the dragon… It sh-shrank down… There was this big whirl…and it became that child…"

"Don't be stupid," Blade said, grabbing the finger Earnest was pointing at him. "Dragons can't turn into people. Use some common sense."

"C'monnn, honored Father, pay *attention* to meeee…" The child behind him began struggling. Apparently, it was a girl. There were two very small but noticeable bumps hitting him on the back.

"Quiet down," he said. "Let's look for your mom and dad, okay?"

"Yes! If you order me to, I shall be quiet. I am willing to obey."

*So she can follow directions. She's actually a pretty cute kid.*

"B-but you know…," said Earnest. "I mean… W-we all saw it… All of us did. Didn't we?"

Everyone nodded.

Blade sighed. "Whatever. We gotta find that dragon or we're in trouble, right? Where did it even go?"

"…Blade?" said Sophie. "Earnest is telling the truth. I saw it as well. That child is the dragon."

"Whaaat?!" Blade was shocked. He took another good look at the child hanging off his back.

"Honored Father! I was quiet for you. I was quiet for ten seconds! Now pay attention to meeee!"

Her brilliant smile was right beside his head. When she grinned like that, he was able to see her sharp fangs. And now that he was paying attention... *Wait, this girl has horns?! Two of them, one on each side of her head... And blond hair? And that pattern covering her body... It looks familiar! It's the same as the yellow dragon that was here just a moment ago!*

"Huh? Hey! Whoa...! What? What *is* this? The dragon? *This* is the dragon? Why is it a little kid now?!"

"That's what I've been trying to tell you!" said Earnest. "Why do you only believe it when *Sophie* tells you?!"

"Honored Fatherrrrr..."

"Wh-why is she calling me her father?!"

"Listen to me when I'm talking!" Earnest shouted.

"Pay attention to meeeee!"

Things were getting out of hand.

## ○ Scene IV: Fatherhood

"It itches right there, honored Father."

"Ah, yeah, sure."

"Oooh... It's so sensitive, right at the base of my horns! Be a bit gentler!"

"Ah, yeah, sure."

Blade was lathering up the girl's hair, as if in a daze. His special dorm room came with a bath, which was a blessing right now. He had filled the water up to half her height in the tub, used soap to bubble it up, and now he was washing her hair.

So much had happened—too much, really—and Blade could no longer react to any of it. He was practically a zombie.

It had been decided that Blade would keep the baby dragon. If they had captured her in dragon form, they could have brought her to some more suitable place, perhaps...but now that she was in human form and capable of speech, the laws of this kingdom classified her as a "person." The horns didn't disqualify her from that right; a sizable minority population of demilings lived in the kingdom, and some of them looked even less like a typical human than she did. Despite the personal shortcomings of its leader, this kingdom was fairly progressive and did not subject its demilings to prejudice or segregation or the like. Blade knew a female centaur—the kind where the horse was the bottom bit—serving as a general in the army, for example.

"You've been washing the same spot for a whole minute now, honored Father."

"Ah, yeah, sure."

He'd finished with her hair. Now it was time to wash her body.

"Ah-ha-ha-ha-ha! You're tickling me, honored Father!"

"Ah, yeah, sure."

Blade had been left in charge of her in no small part because she called him "honored Father" and hounded him like a daughter. But he also served as insurance, in case her dragon side started to stir up trouble again. When it came to people in the capital who could "discipline" a baby dragon, Blade and the king were about all they had.

"I'd like to think this'll work out, but…"

"What do you mean, honored Father?"

"Hey, Cú, you're not gonna get all violent again, right?"

"If you say so, honored Father, I promise never to do it again. That's a dragon promise! Besides, honored Father, it's your fault anyway. You weren't there when I came out of the egg. You're a failure as a parent."

"Ah, yeah, sure," came Blade's halfhearted reply.

The reason this dragon girl insisted on calling him her "honored Father," was thanks in part to these powerful creatures' rather unique life processes. When a dragon hatched from its egg, it was first stomped upon by its parents—a draconic form of discipline meant to show the newborn that it wasn't the strongest creature around. *This* dragon, however, hadn't run into any of her kind before—and although he'd had no idea at the time, Blade had provided the orphaned dragon girl her first "stomping." Naturally, she had imprinted on him.

"That's all right. It's fine. I won't be angry. I finally met you, after all. And you gave me a name, too!"

The dragon hadn't come with a name, and calling her "you" would be inconvenient in the long run. So, as her "parent," Blade had given her one.

"But honored Father, what does the name 'Cú Chulainn' even mean?"

"Mmm? Ah... Well, it's the name of a really powerful knight from a story I heard once long ago."

"Oh. Powerful, huh? I like power!"

"Yeah. He had this super strong sense of duty, and he always kept his promises."

"Oh! Well, I'll keep mine, too. A dragon's promise is more valuable than life itself!"

"Good girl, Cú." He tousled her hair. The sudden shock of becoming a father hadn't yet worn off, and he was still a little spaced out.

"Blade! Blade, are you there?!" He could hear Earnest's voice. It sounded like she wasn't knocking so much as kicking on the door. It wasn't locked, so it swung right open. "Blade! Where are you?!"

She stormed right to the bathroom, her loud footsteps echoing as she searched for him. She stomped right through the door, opened the curtain...and immediately closed it again.

"H-hey!" she shouted, almost screaming. "You moron! If you were in the bath, just *say* so!"

*You didn't give me much time...*

Blade poked his head out from behind the curtain. "Did you learn anything?"

Earnest threw a sheaf of papers on his bed. "Our findings are summarized in this report."

"Can you start with the conclusion?"

"Ugh..."

Cú Chulainn had been constantly clinging to him, refusing to leave his sight, so he had asked Earnest to investigate for him. When it came to dragons, they didn't need the Royal Forbidden Library—consulting regular libraries and scholars would be more than enough.

"Well, it's pretty clear that she's a dragon," said Earnest.

"Yeah, I can see that."

"It *might* have been a girl subjected to dragon-transformation magic, you know."

"Oh, yeah. Sorry."

"D-don't *apologize* all the time, you idiot."

Why did she keep calling him names? Saying sorry, taking a bath—everything he did seemed to make him an idiot.

"First off…dragons taking human form is pretty rare, but as we found out, it's not impossible."

"Mm-hmm."

Blade listened to Earnest talk through the curtain. She was blushing a little (why?) as she sat down on his bed and started skimming the report.

"Magic beasts like dragons are constantly seeking strength. Their bodies dissipate when they're defeated, but part of their soul survives this process and turns into an accumulation of data."

"Oh, right. I heard that it sinks into the earth or something, right? There's this kind of mausoleum deep underground, where their souls get rebuilt."

"You heard that? From whom? Hee-hee… Do you have a magic beast pal or something?" Earnest smiled. Maybe she thought he was joking.

*Ah. I see. Normal people aren't friends with magic beasts, huh? Guess not.*

"And for the record, I've never heard of a theory like that—this 'mausoleum' or whatever you're talking about. None of the researchers I spoke to brought it up."

*Oh. So even the idea is weird. Well, whatever.*

Blade continued washing Cú as he listened to Earnest. Meanwhile, Cú would try to wriggle out of his grasp when he got to certain areas, forcing him to grab onto her and really scrub.

"…Now, since their souls are essentially immortal, when they are reborn, they are sometimes able to mimic the form of whatever defeated them. The victor must have been terribly strong, after all, so by assuming their appearance and qualities, the dragon is trying to evolve into something even stronger. That's the idea anyway. It must be a kind of natural instinct for them."

"So a dragon who was beaten by a person could transform into a person?"

"Exactly. That's what I meant when I said it wasn't impossible. But it almost never happens. No human can defeat a dragon, after all."

*Well, I dunno about that...*

In fact, to Blade, it seemed like nearly everyone could. By "everyone," however, he meant the people he used to know in his Hero days. It had sure *felt* like there were a lot of them...

"Even a baby dragon like that little girl... Apparently a great number of people helped, and they still had to use a trap. Humans may be able to defeat dragons using strategies like that, but for one to want to mimic a human form, the human would have to fight a Great Dragon or an Ancient Dragon one-on-one."

*No, really, there were a ton of people like that around me... Um...*

But, as Blade was starting to realize, those people probably weren't normal. For that reason, he decided not to bring them up.

"Do you think Cú was killed by a human in a previous incarnation?"

Blade had finished bathing the baby dragon while they spoke, and he now picked Cú up from behind and sank her into the tub until the water was at shoulder level. Cú always quieted down when someone else was nearby. She wasn't exactly on guard, she just stared at them, openly hostile.

"Huh? What's Koo? Is that the girl's name? You named her?"

"Yeah. Good name, huh?"

"You idiot. She's not a dog."

"Stop calling me names already." Blade pouted. *I thought it was pretty good.*

Blade got into the tub himself, then thought for a moment as some of the water splashed over the side. Come to think of it, at the age of five—or maybe seven?—he was tossed into a dragon's lair, wasn't he? Back then he hadn't been skilled enough to control his power, and he'd wound up killing a bunch of the creatures. Could *that* episode have something to do with this?

"I've been listening to you two for a while now...," said Cú suddenly. "Did you want to see my dragon form, honored Father? Should I show it to you? It's no big deal for me."

"No." He tousled her wet hair. If she turned back into a dragon now, it'd wreck the bathroom. *And* the building.

"Huh? Whoa! *She's* in there, too?!" Apparently, it had taken Earnest until now to notice.

"Yeah. She's right here."

"You're in the *bath* with her?!"

"Yeah. She won't take a bath by herself, so I have to help—"

The curtain whirled open.

"You, you *freak*!" Earnest shouted.

*That's a pretty impressive front kick*, thought Blade, just as it slammed into his face.

## ○ Scene V: Accusations

"I can't believe this, I can't believe this, I can't believe this..."

The following afternoon, the usual eight members of what was now being called "Earnest's Gang" were all at their usual table, and for some reason, they were all lodging accusations at Blade. Or lashing out. One of the two.

"He was taking a bath with her! I can't believe it! I can't believe it!"

"But... When I put her in alone, all she does is sit there under the showerhead. She doesn't wash herself at all, so I had to..."

He had already defended himself many times. Why weren't any of them accepting such a clearly logical argument? Instead, they all looked at Blade with accusation in their eyes. The glares from the female contingent were particularly fierce.

"Um... This girl... She *does* have...breasts, right?" asked Claire. Claire was the nicest person in the group. *She* would be most likely to understand, he thought.

"Yeah, about this big."

He wasn't sure how this was relevant…but he decided to be as sincere as he could. Using his palms, he attempted to create the form of her very flat, tiny, ever-so-small breasts…

"Ahhhhhhh!"

A close-fisted punch was delivered straight into Blade's face. He didn't bother to dodge. Both this one and Earnest's kick the previous day had come while Cú was sitting on his lap, so he had decided to simply take the hits. He figured if he evaded them, it'd only make the girls even angrier.

"Ahhh! I'm sorry, I'm sorry! Blade?! I, I didn't mean to—"

"It's fine, it's fine. I don't mind."

Blood seeped out from his cut lip. These girls weren't in the senior class of the School for Champions for nothing. It had been a good punch with just the right force behind it—probably enough to kill the average person.

Cú, on Blade's lap, licked up his blood. "Honored Father, I'm hungry," she said. With blood still on her lips, those words sounded especially threatening.

"Then eat. C'mon, open your mouth…"

He picked up some food with a spoon and shoved it into her mouth.

"I can eat by myself, of course. But when my honored Father feeds me, it tastes much better. If you don't even know *that*, honored Father, I believe you may have something a little wrong with your brain. But never fear—even your faults are charming to me."

"Ah, yeah, sure."

He shoved the spoon into her mouth again. That seemed to be the only way to keep her quiet.

"Ah, ah, ah… Ah, me too…" Claire stared at Cú, smitten. She put some of her own food on a spoon and offered it to the dragon girl.

"*Graaah!*" Cú bared her fangs.

"Eek!" Claire pulled back her spoon, shocked and teary-eyed.

"Hey, now." Blade grabbed Cú's head and turned it around so she was looking at him. Then he shoved in another spoonful. It was feeding time.

Cú was sitting on Blade's lap, joining them for lunch, but she seemed somehow detached from her surroundings. She never seemed interested in the others' conversation, even when she was the subject; in fact, she acted like none of the other people around her existed. It seemed she only had eyes for Blade.

Being so adored as a parent was embarrassing. It was a little terrifying, too. She might be taking human form for now, but she was still a dragon. The way she refused to acknowledge anyone weaker than her was proof of that. That was how dragons operated.

"You have become my parent, honored Father, so you have to take good care of me at all times. To be more specific, when you wake me up, you have say 'good morning' and give me a kiss. When we're eating, you have to put me on your lap and feed me. I don't like being carried in your arms, but if you insist, honored Father, I will consider allowing it."

"Ah, yeah, sure." Blade sounded less than enthusiastic.

*I'm doing that right now*, he thought. *You're on my lap and I'm feeding you. So what's the problem?*

"You *do* all that?!"

"What?"

Earnest stood up, distressed. "In...in the morning! Y-you, you *kiss* her...?!"

"No, I don't."

"Oh..." She flopped back into her chair.

"And another thing, honored Father. You keep looking only at mature female bodies. I cannot stand for that. Normally, you'd deserve to be burned to a crisp by my flame breath, but that isn't convenient for me, either, so I'll overlook it. You should be grateful. And rein in your behavior a little, all right? So...to sum up...you have to pay more attention to meeee..."

"Ah, yeah, sure." Blade lifted Cú's arms and waved them around in a little dance.

"F-female bodies...?"

The other "female bodies" at the table turned pale...all except for Sophie.

"Y-you look at our bodies?" Earnest glared at him reproachfully while covering herself defensively with her arms.

"What?" asked Blade. Was there something wrong with the dance he was doing with Cú just now?

"What do you think?" Judge Earnest addressed the other girls.

"Guilty," said Claire. "Totally guilty. There's zero reasonable doubt."

"I think...he's been bad," mumbled Sophie.

"I declare him the worst scum I have ever met," said Yessica.

"Well, then. By a unanimous vote, I hereby declare the defendant guilty of all charges."

Wait, was this a courtroom? This was the first Blade was hearing about it.

## ○ Scene VI: Skill Training

Blade, sentenced to ten thousand years without parole, was standing vacantly in a corner of the Proving Ground. The classes after lunch all involved arena training, something that occupied much of the senior class's time. Blade was never good at listening to lectures anyway; he much preferred training classes, which allowed him to move around and get some exercise.

But today, nobody would team up with him. Some of the boys sympathized and offered to help, but one glare from Earnest sent them running.

Everyone else seemed to be enjoying themselves. They were performing another routine devised by Earnest, where everyone paired up with someone who used a different kind of weapon. For those fighting an opponent they had trouble with, it would teach them how to overcome that disadvantage; those fighting an opponent they had a one-up against would learn how to leverage that advantage to finish the job. This approach provided an opportunity for both, and like Earnest always said, "You can only do in actual battle what you've already done in training."

This really impressed Blade. To tell the truth, he had never trained before. Every day had been actual combat for him—that was the life of a Hero. Now, in his new life as a normal person, he had a lot to learn...but most importantly, he was allowed to make mistakes. That was so wonderful.

When a Hero erred…even in the best-case scenario, it could wipe a town off the map.

*I love training so much…*

As Blade swung his sword all alone, fending off a nearly broken attack automaton that only halfheartedly struck back at him—

"Blade! ♡"

"Hey, hey!"

—Claire and Yessica approached.

"Oh, you guys start today, right?" said Blade. He recalled the cake they had eaten in celebration.

"Yep! We're making our big debut in the senior class!" Yessica excitedly struck a little pose.

"Congrats… Hmm? Hang on."

To Blade, something seemed off about the two of them. He thought about it for a moment…then he thought some more… He looked them up and down over and over, and then it finally dawned on him.

"Oh, you got new outfits."

At long last, he noticed. It all made sense to him now. Anyone else might have overlooked it entirely. They were both wearing their own outfits, not the standard junior class uniforms. They had that freedom now.

"Eek, don't stare at me so closely… You're embarrassing me." Claire was fidgeting a bit. Her new clothing was quite colorful, a big contrast from the monotone uniform. She had shortened her skirt a bit, too.

"Well? What do you think?" asked Yessica, puffing out her chest and twisting her hips.

"It looks cold," said Blade.

"Ah-ha-ha-ha-ha! I love that! I knew you'd say something hilarious, Blade!"

Yessica convulsed a bit as she laughed. She was wearing quite a revealing outfit, almost a swimsuit. It showed off a lot of her brown skin. The short pants she had chosen looked easy to move around in, and the halter top—again, not using much in the way of cloth—emphasized her breasts. Was she aiming to affect her opponents psychologically? Blade had once asked a female warrior why she bothered fighting with bikini armor on. "Because," she had swiftly replied, "it puts men off their guard."

If you told Blade that a woman's chest had the special ability of attracting a man's eye, he likely wouldn't be sure what you meant…but when he and Sophie had been cheek to cheek earlier, it had sent a shock wave through his body. Ever since then, the sight of a cheek, or a pair of lips, had begun to excite him, if only a little.

"Hey! Quit ogling her like that!" said Claire. "Ugh! Yessica, I know you can wear what you want in the senior class, but you don't have to go *that* far!"

"Oh, why not? I like it… If you're curious, Claire, why don't *you* try wearing something more revealing? Right, Blade? Don't you want to see that? She's got considerable assets herself."

"Yeah, I guess so." Blade's gaze was distant.

Glancing around the Proving Ground…he found her. A yellowish figure sitting by herself against the wall. She was all the way over there, watching. It concerned him, as her father.

"I think this one's broken," said Claire, referring to Blade's attack automaton. She walked up to it, reached out…and patted its torso, then two of its four shoulders, then one out of its three legs. A strange glow emanated from the palm of her hand.

"Okay. All set."

With one final pat to its head, the attack automaton started moving around, full of energy. Swinging the blades in all four of its arms, it began to attack the nearest target—Claire. She fended off its attack using a mace with a round, spiky ball at the end.

"See? All better."

"You used your restoration ability?" asked Blade.

Seeing as it could even fix machines, her ability was definitely more "restoration" than "healing." This was neither magic nor a battle skill, but a rare ability that only a few people were gifted with. Powers like hers could come from various sources. Some were innate, others were favors or curses bestowed by supernatural beings. Claire had to be one such person. Blade had never seen anything like it.

"If you get hurt, Blade, tell me, okay? I can restore most things to normal."

"Okay." Blade nodded. She had fixed up his hand before. With her around, he could train without worrying about getting hurt.

"You know…," said Yessica. "I specialize in spy stuff. I'm looking to enter the School of Intelligence." For some reason, she struck a sexy pose.

"Sophie's good at that stuff," commented Blade.

Detecting stuff, picking up on people's presences—that kind of precision work wasn't really Blade's strong suit. Sophie had a much keener sense for it.

"Hey, Soph!"

"…Soph?"

Yessica flew over to Sophie. Blade, watching her back and rear end, sensed a pair of eyes stabbing into the nape of his neck and turned around. It was that yellow figure again—Cú, holding her knees and staring right at him. Or glaring. She *did* just tell him not to stare at mature females back at lunch, didn't she? But Blade figured she was glaring at him for more than just that. Was she jealous, because he was having fun with his friends and she wasn't included?

"Cú! C'mon!" Blade swung his sword toward her. "Wanna join in?!"

Other people noticed his shout. They all focused their eyes on Cú.

Earnest had given careful consideration to her training curriculum, but the other students were still sorely lacking in practice against nonhumans. Fighting someone with (more or less) the same shape as you required a very different approach from fighting a beast several times your size—and it was exactly those types of mismatched battles that they were more likely to encounter. If Cú could transform for them—"baby" dragon or not—she'd be several times their size. It'd make for a great training exercise…

…But Cú just looked away and stood up. She patted the sand off her backside and left.

*Awww...*

Blade was disappointed. Everyone else, however, looked relieved. Maybe they weren't all as enthusiastic about the idea as he was. Unlike Blade, most of the others felt like they had just dodged a bullet.

## ○ Scene VII: At Night

The room was filled with the sounds of light snoring. Cú had finally fallen asleep.

Her small body was taking up half the bed. Blade pulled the blanket up to her shoulders, wrapping her up in it. When he poked at her soft-looking cheek, he was rewarded by her grabbing his finger with her little hand.

*Oh no. Now she's got my finger.*

Blade exhaled deeply as he watched her peaceful sleeping face. She had demanded that he tell her a story, so he had. Most people would take the opportunity to tell a fairy tale of some sort, but Blade didn't know any, so he told her a story about a Hero instead.

"There was once a Hero who carried a sword," he began, "and at the age of three, he faced off against an army of fifty thousand." He kept going until the Hero stormed the Overlord's hideout, and when he informed her that there was no more story after that, she fell asleep. (The sequel to this tale, "The Ex-Hero Goes to School," was still in development.)

The experience taught Blade that stories full of blood and guts made her eyes sharpen and glint. Clearly, they weren't the best choice for a bedtime story. He'd have to ask someone for advice.

*Earnest...? No. She won't know any. I'll ask Claire or Yessica. That sounds like a plan.*

Just then, he heard two knocks on the door. Soft ones, like the knocker wasn't too sure about disturbing him.

"Blade...are you there?"

The voice was almost a whisper, but he could still make it out. Blade never locked his door, so after a few moments, his visitor cracked it open a little.

"Shhh…"

Blade met Earnest's gaze and used a finger to signal that she should be quiet. Then he carefully got up from the bed. He gave one more poke to Cú's cheek, dodging the hands that reached out to grab him, and walked over to Earnest, closing the door behind him as he left the room.

"What is it?" he asked her.

"I don't mean this like *that* or anything. Don't get the wrong idea."

Earnest said the most incomprehensible things sometimes. She didn't mean it like *what*? He'd just asked her a simple question.

"It's about that kid."

*What else would it be about?* Blade thought as he listened.

They walked down the darkened hallway from the boys' dorm to the courtyard so they could be alone. The moons, always shining in the same spot each night, were casting their pale white light on the ground as usual. It made Earnest's tall, slender form stand out in the darkness. Blade stared at her body, a little overcome by how it seemed to shine. Cú would probably yell at him about "mature female bodies" again, but what could he do? Earnest was pretty.

"You know what I want to say, right?" she asked.

"What's that?"

Another glare. If he weren't a former Hero, the look she'd just given him would have stopped his heart.

"You can't pretend to be father and daughter forever."

Oh, that's what this was about? She should have just said so.

"I know," Blade replied.

"No you don't," Earnest shot back immediately. "Besides, how can you take care of a kid at *your* age? In the future, wh-when you get, um, m-married, you'll already have a child. That will cause you all sorts of trouble."

"Why are you stammering? …And why are you worried about *that* of all things? I can't believe you're even thinking that far ahead."

He was expecting something more like *Look, Blade, dragons get really big. How long do you think you can keep her?*

Baby dragons could grow up to a few yards in length, while a Young Dragon could be over ten yards long and a Great Dragon might be several dozen yards. By the time they became Ancient Dragons, they would be much, much bigger—hundreds of yards, even miles long. That was how dragons worked; they kept growing longer and longer. They never stopped.

"I get it, okay?"

He didn't understand the bit about getting married, though… And he didn't know why Earnest even cared. Regardless, he could tell she was worried about him.

"But if I don't act as her father, she'll be all alone in the world."

"……"

Earnest fell silent.

"And you know how hard it is to be alone."

The pain of loneliness, of not having friends—Earnest knew it well, and so did Blade.

"…That's not fair," she said. "You know there's nothing I can say to that."

"Sorry."

"…It's fine. I know you didn't take her in for any *dirty* reasons."

Was *that* it? *That's* what she was worried about? Really?!

"Oh, but show me your back real quick."

"Huh?"

Earnest, her expression a little brighter, suddenly changed the subject. And she'd said something weird, too. Blade was a little taken aback.

"U-um… I'm not really into exhibitionism…"

"You idiot! I wanted to see your wound!"

"Wound? Which one?"

He reluctantly took his shirt off and showed her his back. She traced her finger across his back in the moonlight. It made him feel restless.

"Wow… These really are something. I thought I was seeing things in the bath…but they're really there."

"Those are old. They're all healed up now."

She had described them as "wounds," but really, they were scars. There were countless ones all over his body from his days as a Hero.

"Hey, show me your front, too."

"What, are you gonna ask me to take off my pants next?"

"Idiot!"

She took a look at his chest and stomach. There was a much larger scar there, one quite a bit more recent.

"Oh, *that's*..."

"This one's new...isn't it?"

It was from his encounter with the Overlord. He had nearly died. He'd lost half of his guts, and healing magic couldn't fix him. Without the lady doctor's "medical science," he would have died for sure. Of course, he had inflicted enough wounds on the Overlord that not even dark regeneration skills could repair him, so Blade figured he had still come out ahead. Take *that*, Overlord.

"You...have a past like nothing I could imagine..." He thought her voice sounded a bit lonely.

"Wanna hear about it?" He wouldn't mind telling Earnest. He trusted her.

"In time." Earnest smiled a little, then helped him re-dress.

"Did you know about these...Sophie?" Earnest was looking to the side. Blade, not knowing what was going on, followed her gaze.

"...S-Sophiiiie?!" He was amazed to see Sophie's face floating in the darkness. Her head, ghoul-like under the moonlight, nodded in reply.

"*Tch*... You did, huh?"

"Eeeeeek!" Blade was still in a state of shock, his heart racing.

"Why are you so surprised?" asked Earnest.

"H-how could I *not* be? I didn't sense her at all!"

"She's always like that. What is it? Did you really not know she was there? She's been here the whole time. I ran into her on my way to your room. I guess she wanted to cheer you up, just like me."

*Cheer me up? Who? Earnest? All she did was whine about Cú.*

"Blade. Come here." Sophie spread her arms, then moved them around, as if casting some sort of spell. She'd open them up horizontally, then close them—back and forth, back and forth.

"What?" Earnest looked confused.

Blade smiled wryly. A while ago, he had clung to Sophie's stomach, crying as hard as he could. He had sobbed like a little kid, and Sophie had kept holding him the whole time, like a mother.

"It's all right," he told her.

"Oh." Sophie nodded breezily and stepped back, melting into the darkness. Once again, Blade had no idea if she was still there or not.

"I'm leaving, too." Earnest started to walk away, then turned around and flashed him a smile. "I can't let any anyone see me meeting with a boy late at night, after all."

*She can't? Why not?*

Several question marks danced above Blade's head as he saw her off.

## ○ Scene VIII: Late Night Cú

When Blade returned to his room, Cú was gone. All that was left was her impression on the blanket.

"Huh?"

Blade looked around for her. He felt a breeze and realized the window was open.

Holding back the flapping curtains, he leaned outside. Had she gone up, or down? Probably up—that's what his gut told him.

Grabbing the window frame, he swung his body out and up, as if performing the beginning of a back hip circle. He changed position midair, landing safely with his feet on the roof. Cú was sitting there, in the almost-blinding moonlight.

"What's wrong, Cú?" He approached her and sat down a short distance away.

"It calms me, looking at them."

"The moons?"

Cú was looking at the two unevenly sized circles hanging in the sky.

"The bigger one is the parent, and the smaller one is the child. That's why they're always together."

"I'm not sure it's anything that romantic, Cú. Some people say those are a couple of holes opened up in the ceiling of—"

"When I was alone in the wilderness, I watched them a lot."

"Ah..." Blade clammed up. He'd said the wrong thing.

He moved to sit closer to her, so they were almost touching. He wanted to apologize with his behavior, rather than his words.

Quietly, Cú placed her head on his shoulder. "You seem to worry about me, honored Father. About how I don't have any friends."

"Ah..."

*I guess the cat's out of the bag on that one.*

"But you needn't worry," she said, looking up at the moons. "Dragons possess bodies and spirits far more powerful than those of humans. I don't know what worries you exactly, honored Father, but dragons aren't in the habit of forming packs. We live alone, and we die alone. That's how we are. So I am perfectly fine."

Then Cú took her eyes off the moon and turned them toward Blade. Her vertical slitted pupils were open wide as she looked at him.

"Besides...I have you, honored Father. Isn't that enough?" She rubbed her head against Blade's side.

Blade was ashamed of himself. As parent, how could he make his child worry about him?

"You sure are strong, Cú." He patted her head. But stroking her hair didn't feel like a big enough expression of his love, so he began to rub and knead her scalp.

"That's a little too hard, honored Father." Blade, his worries gone, kept rubbing Cú's head. "Oh, honored Father, you're hopeless."

## ○ Scene IX: Playing Alone

The bell rang across the Proving Ground, signaling the end of afternoon class.

*Oh, we're done already?*

Blade looked around, tapping his shoulder with his wooden sword. He didn't feel like he had worked hard enough yet. The other students were making their way off the field, shouting, "Ahhh, it's finally over," and the girls were griping about the Empress's strenuous training regimen on their way to the showers.

"You look like you want some more, Blade." Earnest was smiling at him.

"Yeah," he said. "I kind of do."

Compared to his first few days at school, when he was still recuperating, he was feeling a lot healthier now. After the doctor had examined every inch of his body (including the inside of his bowels), she had officially given him permission to break out up to 30 percent of his full force.

"But I guess everyone's already leaving."

"Did you want to stay for some extra training? I'll join you."

Had he sounded that reluctant to leave? Earnest had worked the senior class to the bone that day (or so the other students said), and yet here she was, acting like she was just hanging out doing her own thing. Blade already knew that once she was done working over the other students, she stayed behind on the Proving Grounds, training by herself.

"Want me...to help?"

Blade's heart skipped, and he whipped around at the sound of Sophie's voice. He really wished she wouldn't stand around, completely undetectable.

"Um...well," he said. "I'd appreciate it, but..."

If he had two partners, they could accomplish a lot with the time they had. But Blade decided to bow out. He needed to go pick up his daughter soon.

"Ah, yes... I bet His Majesty is having a rough time of it." Earnest nodded.

During lectures, Cú would sit obediently in Blade's lap, but that didn't work on the Proving Ground. He kept inviting her to join in, but she'd always refuse and go sit in a corner. To Blade, it felt like abuse to make her wait there all day.

For that reason, he'd arranged to have someone watch her while he trained. And that "someone" was the very man Earnest had mentioned—the king. A dragon, after all, wouldn't accept anyone weaker than itself. And even though Cú was a baby dragon, the only humans stronger than her were Blade and the king.

"Okay, I'm gonna go pick her up…," said Blade.

He waved to the two of them before heading off.

## ○ Scene X: Chancellor's Office

"What exactly do you think I am?"

The moment Blade opened the door to the chancellor's office (without knocking, of course), the king started complaining. He shoved his pile of paperwork off to the side, took off his glasses, and glared directly at Blade—hard enough that even Earnest could probably learn a thing or two from it. When the king first met Cú, he'd made her admit defeat with one of those glares alone.

Blade shrugged off the look with a breezy wave. Its power was knocking books off the shelf behind him, but he paid this no mind. It's not like *he'd* be cleaning that up.

"I would like you to stop using the king's office as a nursery."

"This is the *chancellor's* office. *You're* the one bringing in your king work."

"Look at me, being made to look after a child. Hah! In the fifty years since I was born as your king, I've never been treated this way."

"Don't be stupid. You weren't *born* king. You were just a prince back then."

Blade didn't feel a shred of guilt. Back when he was a Hero, the king had him attending to his every whim. This didn't even come close to paying off that debt. And besides, he was the one who had thrown Blade into this school in the first place. Just look at him now—he'd fired the old chancellor, taken his spot, and was now leaning back in his chair, acting like the boss of everyone… He'd told Blade to get to know other girls and boys his age and use the experience to regain his powers. He must be crazy. And come to think of it, what was a Hero supposed to do with no Overlord to fight? Who'd want to take that job? Stupid, stupid, stupid.

"I can hear you, you know."

"Oh? Did I say that out loud? Oopsie."

"You can think whatever you want about me. My love for you has never changed."

"S-stop that! I *hate* that sort of talk!"

"Ha-ha-ha! You'd prefer it from a woman, I suppose? I'm sure you would. You would, wouldn't you? I bet you've already won a few hearts."

"Quit it, you rotten old man. Stop measuring young people by the standards of *your* generation."

"Ah-ha-ha! They called me the stud horse of the continent, you know."

"First time I'm hearing it."

Blade looked around the room. Cú wasn't there. He wondered if a game of hide-and-seek was in progress, but he couldn't sense her presence, either.

"By the way, where's Cú?"

"Would you believe it? I had her on my lap here, giving her a *pat, pat, pat, pat* on the head, and she started whining about it. When I said 'Aw, that's cute' and started rubbing my chin against her, she got even more upset. 'Your beard whiskers,' she said, 'they're too spiky. They hurt. Is that supposed to be an attack? An attack?'"

"I thought you hated looking after children."

"So I went to have a quick shave, and the next thing I knew…"

"…Cú bolted because you were doting on her too much and she got sick of it? You can't even watch a little kid, can you? Ugh. Useless."

"Ahhh, it does feel nice to be lectured for a change… Feel free to rebuke me more if you like."

"I can't believe you don't even know how to spoil grandkids at your age. You have to leave them be until they nestle up to you. That always does the trick."

"Oh, really? A valuable lesson, indeed!"

"Useless."

Giving up on the king, Blade left the room. He asked several students if they'd seen Cú, then followed the leads he was given...all the way back to his own dorm room.

He could sense her the moment he cracked open the door. He slid inside, relieved.

"Now, now, now! No picking on a young dragon like that. Have you no pity?"

He could hear an affected voice, like an actor in a play. It belonged to Cú. She must have been playing by herself.

Sneaking up ever so carefully to take a peek, he found Cú holding a doll in a vise grip, talking to herself and playing. Another doll was in her other hand; she was doing a little show where one of the dolls attacked the dragon plush on the floor and the other one defended it.

*Aha. So that was one of the dolls speaking just now.*

"Oh! Blade! No, I wasn't bullying it at all! *Glare!*"

"You fool! I will not abide such lies!"

"Huuuh? Oh no! My super eye beam...!"

Earnest's super eye beam wasn't working, apparently. So one doll was Earnest, and the other was Blade.

"No bullying! Ever! You're so stupid, Earnest. *Whack! Whack! Whack!*"

"Oh noooo! I'm sorry, I'm sorry! I won't do it again!"

Blade had a taste for domestic violence, it seemed.

"As long as you understand. As long as you understand..."

"Ohhh, but you're sooo strong! I love you! I want to lay your egg!"

"You fool! I would never accept a weak female like you!"

Blade had dumped her. *Also, "egg?" Please don't rewrite biology on me.*

With a grin, the real Blade decided it was about time to speak up...but then he froze up, shocked. There was a crate beside Cú, filled to the brim with dolls. Not just two or three, but several dozen, at least.

Cú tossed the Earnest doll aside and grabbed another one.

"Ohhh, would you please befriend my daughter?"

"Roger. No prob."

She assumed a neutral expression as she spoke, so Blade figured this was probably meant to be Sophie. For some reason, he could just tell. This doll, too, was soon tossed away, and she grabbed a fourth.

"Ohhh, if you will become my daughter's friend, I shall give you my seed!"

*I would not. I'm not giving anyone anything.* What did she even mean, "seed"?

"Cú, Cú... *Pat, pat, pat, pat, pat, pat, pat...*"

"No fair, Claire! I want to pat her too. *Pat, pat, pat, pat, pat, pat...*"

"Shut *up*, all of you!"

Suddenly, the plush dragon roared its disapproval. It must be shy.

"Aww, what a darling girl. I love all women!"

Oh, wait, that had to be Leonard, didn't it? Blade felt pretty sure.

Cú continued taking dolls out from the crate and making them promise to be friends with the dragon plush. Blade cracked a smile.

*Look at her. She acts all tough, but she really does want friends, doesn't she? I really oughta do something about that...*

But as time passed, his face stiffened up. This little play didn't seem to be ending anytime soon. Was she going through the entire junior class, maybe? She must be. Cú knew all of their names, including quite a few Blade didn't even remember. She even imitated their voices, though he suspected there was a lot of fabrication going on, too. She went through all one hundred of them. The whole crew.

*Oh man.*

Blade left his room and wandered the hallways. He was still in shock, but he managed to hide his presence and escape without Cú noticing.

He kept walking, no particular destination in mind. *Cú... Cú... I had no idea she wanted friends that badly... She...she said she was fine being alone... And I believed her...! I didn't even notice! What have...what have I...*

"Blade...? What's up?"

He thought he heard Earnest's voice float into his consciousness from somewhere. But he didn't have time for her right now.

"Did you find Cú yet? No? Want me to search for her, too? Or...you know, it'd be kinda nice to look for her together. ♡"

"I..."

"Mmm?"

"I... I..."

"Wh-whoa, what's wrong?"

"I...! I! Iiiiii...!"

Blade rammed his head into the wall. He kept going, again, and again, and again...

"S-stop! Stop, you idiot! Quit it! You're bleeding! You're hurting yourself!"

Again, and again, and again, and again. The stone wall was the first to give. When that happened, Blade began banging his head against another wall. More, and more, and more.

*I'm such a stupid, stupid, stupid idiot. I'm an idiot!*

"No! No, Blade! No! Stop!"

Instead of his head being punished by the stone, it was now being blocked by something gnarled and rough, so Blade finally stopped.

It was...a pair of red hands. The hands were red. Their fingers, much thinner than his own, were stained in red. They were injured.

"Blade..."

It was Earnest. Blade finally realized that Earnest was there. Since when?

"You... Your hands... They're hurt..."

"You're so stupid, Blade! So stupid!"

Earnest was shouting. Her hands must have hurt, too, but she didn't seem to care at all... Why didn't she care?

"What happened?" she asked. "What's wrong? Tell me, so I can understand!"

Earnest placed both of her injured hands on Blade's cheeks, and Blade nodded back at her.

○ **Scene XI: Courtyard**

"Cú needs friends."

Blade was seated on the edge of the fountain. A bandage-like piece of cloth, torn from Earnest's clothing, was wrapped around his forehead, while Blade had clumsily fashioned similar dressings for Earnest's hands.

He explained to her what he had seen in his room. Earnest listened, her eyes wide. Eventually, when tears began to roll down her cheeks, Blade felt sure she'd understood.

"Cú needs friends," he repeated.

"Yes… You're right." Earnest nodded.

"But she can't help her own instincts. That's why it won't work."

"Calm down, okay? Let's take this step-by-step. Why won't it work? What can't we do for her?"

"If… If you want her to recognize you as her friend, you have to defeat her. Those are her dragon instincts, and there's nothing we can do. She can't accept anyone weaker than her as an equal. But only me and the king are strong enough…"

Blade was deeply troubled. He wanted to do something for Cú, but…

"But I don't have anything to offer. There's nothing I can do."

"Yeah. There's nothing *you* can do about that."

Blade looked up at Earnest. She got to her feet and brought a hand to one curvy hip like she was taunting him. It was a little much, given the circumstances.

"I'm sorry… Can you lay off for now?"

"Will you admit it, then? Will you admit that you can't do anything by yourself?"

"Yes," he said. He admitted defeat to the spirited girl before him. Then he looked down at his feet.

"All right… In that case, you can rely on me."

"Huh?"

"You can't solve this by yourself, right? So rely on me instead. I relied on you not long ago, didn't I? Regarding *this*." She pointed to the sword at her hip.

"Oh, shut *up*!" she said suddenly. "Ugh!"

Reacting to some silent joke, she whacked the sword against the ground a few times. By now this had become standard behavior for Earnest.

"...It's not fair," she said. "I rely on you, but you never rely on me. It's not *right*! I will not stand for such arrogance!"

"U-um... I don't think that has anything to do with being fair..."

"It's *fine*, all right?! Just shut up and rely on me! Rely on *us*!"

Blade examined her face for a few moments. Then, after a pause, he smiled.

## ○ Scene XII: Junior Class

When first period began, Blade visited the junior class. He knew they'd be at the Proving Ground working on their fundamentals.

"One... Two... One... Two..."

Everybody swung their wooden swords at the instructor's call—dozens of boys and girls, lined up and wearing the same uniform, performing the same action. It was an odd sight, made all the odder by the unisex uniforms. In the senior class, everyone wore whatever they wanted, whether red, blue, green, or rainbow-colored. Here, it was monotone black and white.

Blade had been one of them not long ago. To him, however, it seemed like forever. He felt tremendously awkward.

"Why are you following me?" he asked Earnest.

"Why...?" She shot him a blank look. "Because I'm your partner, aren't I?" She said this like it was obvious.

*Wow, really? Since when? Also, what does she mean by "partner"?*

He couldn't ask Earnest any of that right now, however, because she was bashing Asmodeus against the ground again. It was a shame he couldn't hear the intelligent sword's sarcastic remarks. He was starting to feel like he was missing out on some great comedy.

The students seemed to take notice of Blade, and they stopped their incessant swinging. Though when Blade followed their line of sight, it appeared the one who had really drawn their attention was Earnest.

"You stand out too much," he said to her.

"Do I?"

The Empress appeared blissfully unaware as the two of them stood in front of the junior class, sidling past the now-frozen instructor. All eyes were focused on a single point now. Everyone was looking at Blade—not Earnest, just Blade.

Now that he was the center of attention, Blade placed his hands and knees on the ground and lowered his upper body. This was called "kowtowing" in the far reaches of the eastern lands, and it signaled utmost sincerity.

The gesture sent a stir through the crowd, and students began to chatter. With his head against the ground, Blade couldn't see his audience, but their unrest was palpable.

He continued kowtowing and began to speak.

"I need your help!"

"Um… I dunno how we can help you…," came a dubious voice from the crowd.

It was a sensible thing to say. If someone kowtowed to Blade out of nowhere, he'd be just as flummoxed. But he had to get his feelings across to everyone, because he couldn't accomplish this by himself. That was why he was doing this.

"I need your help!" he said again.

"Please," came Earnest's voice from his side.

"Huh?" Blade forgot all about kowtowing and looked over. Earnest was on her knees, hands on the ground and forehead grinding against the stone. She was doing it now, too.

…*She would never! How is this real?*

Getting Earnest to say "please," seemed impossible enough. Now she was kowtowing to a crowd? It defied logic.

"What're you doing?" he asked.

"Kowtowing, Blade."

"I know, but—"

"Get back down."

"Okay."

Blade reassumed his previous position. He had no idea why Earnest was doing this, but as long as she was, he had to keep going, too.

The noise from the junior class grew louder and showed no signs of abating. Soon, it had become a low roar. Blade really wanted to know what was going on, but with his head on the ground, he couldn't see.

Someone else came along, though he could only see her boots.

"I humbly ask you as well."

It was Sophie's voice. Blade shot his head up, looking closely at her face.

"What're you doing?" he asked.

"Kowtowing, Blade."

"Yeah, but—"

"Get back down."

"Okay."

Blade put his head back down. He could sense Sophie next to him, along with a few more people approaching.

"Please, everyone."

"Do it for him."

"Come on."

"We're begging you here."

Claire, Yessica, Clayde, and Kassim joined in. Even more people had shown up—the exact number of students in the senior class, in fact.

*What's going on? I guess the whole senior class is doing this now. And in front of the juniors...*

Blade had come here to make a personal request. He had kowtowed because he knew how ridiculous his plea would sound when he said it. But then Earnest, Sophie, Claire and the gang, and finally the rest of the senior class had joined him. Why?

"Please, get up!" someone in the junior class shouted. "We'll do whatever you want!"

Soon, the voice was joined by dozens of others.

## ○ Scene XIII: Day of Destiny

The big day had arrived. Around a hundred students were on the Proving Ground, facing a lone dragon.

Morale was high on both sides. They had spent a full two weeks preparing for this, and the humans had undergone intense training. Their entire class curriculum had been rearranged just for this purpose. The dragon, meanwhile, had gotten plenty of rest. The word "training" wasn't in a dragon's dictionary. They were all-powerful from birth, and to them, trying to be even stronger was nothing short of cowardice.

Blade had once had the opportunity to speak with a dragon elder. Since they were so strong at birth, he had said, if they trained any more, it would be unfair to the other races. Such was the pride and arrogance of dragons. And while Cú was an orphan, that way of thinking still ran deep in her blood. So, instead of training like the humans, the dragon rested and ate well. For the past two weeks, Cú (having reverted to her dragon form) had been eating one full-grown cow per day. Eat, sleep, eat, sleep. That was how dragons worked. To them, conditioning meant consuming as much nutrition as possible.

The humans, meanwhile, were similarly well prepared.

"Okay, everyone! Let's do it!!"

"Yes, Empress!"

Everyone shouted in unison at Earnest, their weapons held high in the air. She and Blade had thoroughly drilled everyone in what they needed to do. The student body, and no one else, had to beat the dragon that day, and—baby or not—she was a *real* dragon. If a dragon took the fight seriously, even a hundred royal knights would have difficulty besting it in a fair fight. Normally, they'd try to ensnare it in a trap instead. With the right siege weaponry and a skillful plan, it wasn't too hard to finish off even the strongest of creatures without suffering any casualties.

Nobody was stupid enough to try fighting a dragon head-on…but that was exactly what Blade had asked them to do, his head lowered in a bow.

"I need you to fight and defeat the dragon!" he had said, groveling in front of the juniors. "Please be friends with my daughter!"

Not a single member of the student body could sit out. There were exactly a hundred and eight dolls in Cú's toy chest, and now there was exactly that number of students in the arena. They had all gladly accepted the request, and Blade was sure it wasn't just because they thought Cú was cute. He wasn't sure what moved each of them to step up. All he could do was plead with them.

He had participated in their training as well, though he couldn't join the actual battle. If he personally led the students to victory, it wouldn't be enough to change Cú's mind. But if one hundred of them could beat her without him, he felt certain that Cú would acknowledge their strength.

Humans harnessed their fullest potential in groups. To dragons, that did not count as "cowardice." A swarm of bees was much more threatening than a single one, and that was how dragons saw humans as well.

If they could convince her of humanity's strength, then she should be able to accept them as friends. Cú had already been caught by humans once, but back then, apparently, there had been no battle. She was trapped, unable to move, and put to sleep using a mix of drugs and magic. Cú was still in a huff about it.

This time, however, he had told her that she could fight as hard as she wanted. "Go ahead," Blade had said, "test the students out all you like." What truly convinced her, however, was what he said right at the end: "Show them how strong you are." Now she was raring to go.

"Hey. Hey, don't get too worked up, okay? There you go…"

Blade approached Cú and stroked her neck as she spouted little puffs of flame. He was in something of a delicate position here. He had led the human side in their training, but right now, he was in Cú's corner. Once the battle began, he'd be back on the humans' side. He had discussed this with her in advance, and she was all right with it—"show me any mercy," she told him, "and I'll kill you, honored Father."

But…

Blade looked over his shoulder at the VIP seating high up in the arena.

The king was there, hosting a party with some of his beautiful attendants, drinking up a storm as they watched this 1 versus 108 battle.

*What's he even doing? Eesh. This isn't a show.*

"Hey, Cú, while you're fighting, could you accidentally shoot a fireball up there for me?"

Blade pointed at the king. Cú, unable to speak human language in her current form, nodded back.

"All right. I'm heading out. Good luck."

After giving her a few final pats on the neck, Blade moved back toward the other students.

"Are you all ready?"

"We can start anytime," Earnest replied, all 107 students behind her steeling themselves for what was to come. They had received grueling training from the Empress for the past two weeks, turning each one into a seasoned elite. Their morale was nothing short of magnificent.

"Okay! Let's begin!"

The king sat up in his throne-like seat, waving one hand for some reason. Blade chose to ignore him. This was their battle, and they'd decide when it began and when it ended.

And so, without any particular signal or command, the fight commenced.

## ○ Scene XIV: Battle

The fight was underway, but still in its preliminary stages. Blade had moved to a position where he could oversee the entire battlefield…next to the king, much to Blade's chagrin.

"Looks like they're struggling down there, doesn't it?" the king observed between swigs of wine. Whenever his golden goblet was empty, a stunning beauty was always on hand to fill it up with some amazing vintage.

"Shut up, you drunk."

But they—the students—were indeed struggling. Only a few minutes had passed, and two platoons were already trying to flee the fight. Blade and Earnest had divided them into ten or so groups, each composed of around ten people and mostly (but not all) led by a member of the senior class. Individual strength, unfortunately, did not always translate into good leadership.

"Ooh, look, I think another one's about to drop out."

The king didn't need to point this out to Blade. He could see it. Whether it was getting trampled by a front leg or sent flying by a tail whip, multiple students were getting knocked out with a single attack. Only a third of the platoon in question was still in fighting shape; it was no longer functioning as a group.

Blade's job was to keep abreast of the flow of battle and communicate any instructions he saw fit to Earnest. Two platoons were out of the fight, but for now he didn't have any comments. Everything was going as they predicted it would. The survivors from the lost platoons were absorbed by other groups, just as they had been trained. It would be wrong to assume they could take on a dragon and emerge without any casualties. The humans had factored that inevitability into their strategy.

"Ahhh... There goes another. What are they even doing?"

As the king looked on, the third platoon fell, overrun and fleeing for their lives. Nobody had actually died—Cú must've been going at least a *little* easy on them. There were a lot of serious injuries, however. A three-tier medical team—consisting of the doctor, some healers, and Claire with her restoration ability—was on hand, putting triage tags on the wounded and taking care of them. Anyone hurt badly enough to need "restoring" instead of healing was handled by Claire. The people with less serious wounds were handled with regular healing magic or medical procedures. Anyone with non-serious injuries was directed to rub some spit on it and get back out there.

"Were those cards your idea?" asked the king. "The red, yellow, green, and black ones?"

"Huh? Oh. Nah, that was Earnest. It makes it easier to handle the wounded."

"Mmm. She certainly *is* a talent. We'll have to adopt that in the military."

Soon, the battle's opening phase was wrapping up. Now they were getting into the meat of it. Two or three platoons had been knocked out before they could get used to the necessary movements, but the ones that survived quickly learned how to work together to avoid any "accidents" that might wipe out a whole team at once. Despite this, one or two people were wounded every thirty seconds or so. They couldn't afford to let their guard down for a moment.

"Good," said the king. "Very good. This is exactly the sort of training I was picturing for them. How much more practical can you get, I ask you?"

"You like it? Good for you."

Blade was too focused to say much else. His mind was on the battlefield below; he was fighting right alongside them.

There were still ten or so platoons active. About two dozen people had retired from battle, and the ones who were mobile again after being healed were cheering from outside the arena. That was about all they could do now; the rule they worked out with Cú was that if a human was injured to the point they could no longer fight, they'd be healed and then banned from rejoining the battle. They might be all better after healing or restoration, but they couldn't tag back in.

They'd reached the midpoint of the fight. It had mostly gone to plan so far; a few more casualties than anticipated, but nothing they hadn't accounted for. They weren't going to dramatically improve everyone's strength in just two weeks, after all. The main thrust of their special training had been learning how to cooperate. If only one group struck at a time, they could easily be wiped off the map with a single blow—that was how much stronger a dragon was than a human. So two or three platoons needed to constantly be attacking at the same time. That was what they had trained for.

The strength of each team, naturally, varied quite a bit. There was a notable difference between the best and the weakest, and even the most powerful team could be wiped out if they got unlucky. One of the three downed platoons, in fact, was one Blade had deemed their second strongest.

But no matter how many teams were knocked out, the students were organically switching formations, filling in missing spaces, and doing whatever jobs needed to be done. They had trained extensively for that purpose; in fact, it was fair to say they had devoted nearly all of their training time to it. No matter how much damage they took, no matter which team got clobbered, they continued to function as a cohesive force. Each team served as the head, the arms, *and* the legs of their force, just as they had trained.

As the midgame approached its conclusion, their skillful teamwork and formation began to bear some fruit. Slowly, in fits and starts, they began dealing blows to the dragon. But—again, as predicted—they didn't have much effect. You really needed dragon-destroying skills to do critical damage to this kind of creature. A formation like the one the students were employing was mostly meant to buy time while the *real* attackers charged up their moves or cast intricate magic strong enough to penetrate a dragon's tough skin.

But, of course, nobody in the student body was capable of that level of offense. There would be no climactic blow instantly ending the fight. The students' attacks hardly even damaged the dragon's armor; all they did was irritate Cú even more.

For a while, their teamwork seemed to give them the advantage, but gradually, fatigue began to set in. Faced with a dragon's near-infinite endurance, the human's team-based edge began to lose its luster.

"So this is how it ends, eh?" said the king. "Well, *that's* boring. What do you think? How about I take command? I could certainly make things a lot more interesting."

The king was babbling again.

*Save your ravings for someone else. This is our battle.*

But…well…still…the king *was* a talented commander. He had even led the united human forces in the fight against the Overlord's hordes.

Blade nodded to the beautiful women around the king, silently asking them to keep him distracted. They got the message quickly and began ganging up on him.

"Your Maaajesty, look! Look at my breasts!"

"Boobs, boobs, boobs!!"

The king quieted down after that. *Man. Adults are the worst.*

Despite the interruption, Blade was still focused on the battle. The students were digging in and holding out, advancing and retreating like ocean waves in order to keep the dragon in check. With up to three teams engaging her at once, there was always another team behind the attackers. The dragon had no time to rest and gather herself—and being a baby dragon with little fighting experience, she had never faced this much of a challenge before. Her anger and irritation led to mistakes, opening up holes that the students never missed.

That said, the humans were still outclassed in terms of offense. Almost nothing they threw at Cú did any damage. The junior class's students were good enough to *maybe* cut through metal armor with a metal sword. And the senior class couldn't do much better—they could potentially cut through armor made of magical metal with a regular blade. The durable skin of a dragon was tougher than even magic armor.

The only exception—the only people dealing decisive blows—were the very best of the senior class—Earnest, Sophie, Leonard, and so on. Their strikes were precise, landing right as the other students created holes in the dragon's defense for them. Even now Leonard's drill lance was spewing huge amounts of flames as it plunged ahead. Its tip—the drill tip, that is—collided with the dragon's side. Sparks flew as it stabbed several times, then several dozen times. Then the drill was pulled back. It had dealt at least some amount of damage, moving a bit farther into its target with every drill rotation.

"*Graaaaah!*"

The dragon roared and spat out a fan of flames. Leonard and the other students were already out of its blast range. But even after all that, they'd only managed to scratch her. To a human, it was about equivalent to a scraped knee. Put a bandage on it and you were done. Hardly lethal. Now that the humans had stubbornly attacked her dozens of times, Cú was covered in such "Band-Aid level" wounds.

Meanwhile, anytime a student was hit, it knocked them right out of the game. The flame breath was especially potent. If you got caught up in that, *maybe* Claire could restore you, but nothing else could. And nobody wanted to test out whether her restoration skills would work on a pile of ash.

The dragon roared again. It was gradually thinning out the human army, but they were still working together to keep attacking her. The students were facing the strongest beast in the known world, and all they could do was prick, prick, prick until the end of time. Blade had once heard from one of the Overlord's generals that the thing he hated the most about humans was how they never gave up. Each individual was a weakling, but they never threw in the towel. It just wasn't in their nature.

"Ohhh, Your Majesty, that's simply not allowed! You can't! Hands off!"

"Aw, come on, what's the harm?"

Strange voices could be heard from behind Blade. It would be a scandal if the king were married, but he was still single even though he was middle aged. Blade avoided looking back at him and stayed focused on the scene ahead.

Finally, Blade stood up. It was *juuust* about time. He readied his left hand. According to the strategy they'd worked out in advance, Blade had two signals to give to the students—one with his left hand, the other with his right. He couldn't join the fight, but being up in the audience let him see certain things the students couldn't. Things that weren't clear to Earnest and Sophie as they led their platoons and fought on the ground were as clear as day to Blade as a noncombatant.

So he lifted his arm high, then swung it down. He'd just given the first signal—and it put his friends in red and blue on the move.

Earnest and Sophie detached from their respective platoons and began moving by themselves. The top two fighters on the human side promptly put all their focus into attacking. Flashes of red and blue streaked across the arena, taunting the dragon. They constantly changed their position, virtually dancing in front of the dragon as they fought. When the colors crisscrossed, they created strange bursts of light around them, no doubt dazzling Cú's eyes.

She might have nearly infinite endurance, but she was still just a baby with little in the way of mental fortitude. She wasn't relying on intelligent thinking, simply lashing out at whatever irritated her the most. What little prudence and logical thinking she still had was about to abandon her. She turned into a brute animal, just chasing around whatever was in front of her.

That was what Sophie had been waiting for. She ran out into the open and stood there defenseless—all but begging to be trampled. With a piercing roar, the dragon stomped up to her, thinking about nothing but how wonderful it would be to squish her. Cú would have been more careful at the beginning of the fight, but this was the endgame, and the stress had piled up. The humans had yet to land a decisive blow all day. The dragon had seen them in action, and what she saw told her that this opponent was nothing at all to worry about.

So she advanced. Sophie didn't run. And just when it looked like her frail body was about to be crushed—the ground gave way. The dragon, Sophie, and the dirt around them all went hurtling into the space below. It was a pitfall, and the dragon had stepped right into it.

"How is that different from trapping her?" the king asked.

"That—" Blade turned around to answer, then hurriedly spun back after witnessing all the exposed skin around the king. "That wasn't a trap set in advance. They've been digging it ever since the battle began."

"They dug it?"

"Isn't that what a drill's meant for in the first place?" Blade grinned.

Leonard had been absent from the front line for a while now. He hadn't bowed out due to injury, though—and everyone could now see that there was a hole in the arena's ground, just big enough for a person. Another hole suddenly opened up next to it, revealing the dashing lancer caked in mud from head to toe. He had excavated the soil beneath the surface, but not so much that a person's weight would cave it in. No, it would take a dragon to make the ground collapse, and collapse it did.

The dragon struggled to clamber out of the hole. It had been dug quickly and wasn't all that deep. Cú's front legs were already on the lip of the hole as she tried to climb out—and that's when the all-out attack began. An ax wielder, carrying an ax bigger than his own body, swung down with all his might on one finger of her clawed hand.

"*Arrrrrgh!*"

That had to hurt. At least as much as a badly stubbed toe. And they kept it up. Every time the dragon tried to climb out, the students would attack her front legs.

"Hmm... So you were attempting to lure her into a pitfall, eh? ...But it'll take more than that to win, won't it? What do you plan to do now?"

The king, a born commander, was analyzing the situation. But he wasn't commanding this fight. This battle belonged to Blade and the other students...and to Cú Chulainn, his daughter.

"Sorry, Cú," he muttered as he watched his child struggle. *Forgive me. They say a lion isn't afraid to drop its cub into the abyss...and I guess that's what I'm doing to you.*

"I'm not sure they say anything like that, if memory serves..."

The king was babbling again.

*Shut up, old man. I told you, this is our battle. Just shut up and keep drinking. You didn't even show up in Cú's doll theater.*

Blade quietly kept watching, waiting for the right moment to send the second signal.

"It *still* hasn't come?!"

Earnest was increasingly impatient. Blade still hadn't given the second signal. Cú was struggling to get out of the hole, and every time, they pushed her back in—but it took a grueling effort. It was decided in their strategy session that they'd keep this up until Blade gave the signal. Earnest was a soldier right now, and soldiers were obligated to follow orders.

"Yaaaaah!!"

So she swung Asmodeus, throwing out fireballs that burned Cú's legs and sent her back into the hole.

"Leonard! You still good?!" she asked the boy next to her.

She couldn't recharge her flame attack in time for the next round. Leonard would have to take over.

"Yes, milady! I can still hold out. I've been running 10K every morning, like you told me to."

"Huh?"

*Did I say that?* Earnest thought.

But then, just as Leonard readied his next blow, he fell to his knees.

*Oh, great. He folded. All bark and no bite, huh? Useless.*

"Asmodeus! Can you do this?!" She turned to her sword next. She knew she was asking the impossible, but she needed to strike Cú again the next time around.

*"I may have ample heat, but continuing to draw on it like this..."*

"Just give me a yes or no!"

*"No."*

*Why are all men so worthless?*

"Hyaaah!"

Just then, a girl ran in from the side and sent a spiky mace crashing down upon Cú's arm. It was Claire. She was supposed to be manning the medical unit, but now she was armed and running into the fray. The mace must not have hurt that much, however, because all it did was push one of Cú's claws back a little.

"Yah!" Yessica stormed in next, carrying a metal battle fan—an unusual weapon. The fan curved in the air, forming a sharpened blade that cut off one of Cú's claws.

"Claire! Yessica!" Earnest shouted. *Ah, women. They're so much more reliable.*

"Anna!" called Yessica. "Leave this to us! Get yourself ready!" Earnest no longer minded the nickname. "Blade's signal is coming real soon! I'm sure of it!"

"Got it!" Leaving the front line to Claire and Yessica, Earnest returned to her original position. She pointed her sword toward the sky.

"It's time! ...Asmodeus! Don't make me regret becoming your master!"

*I shall do my best.*

She crammed every last drop of her power into the blade. A gigantic fireball began to form.

Blade watched the battle unfold, his mind serene. Over and over again, Cú was being pushed back into the hole.

*Forgive me, Cú. They say a lion isn't afraid [etc.]*

Simply falling back in didn't damage her at all, of course. But Blade knew his daughter well. He knew she wouldn't put up with this for long—and that's what he was watching for right now. If she couldn't crawl out from the hole, what would she do next? She was a dragon, mind you, not some earthbound human. With wings like hers, what strategy would she take?

*"Arrrrrrgh!"* Cú roared, then fanned out her wings.

Blade's eyes opened just as wide.

"Earnest! Now!!"

Earnest was manifesting a gigantic fireball, as big as she could possibly control. She made it as hot as her strength allowed, ignoring Asmodeus's

griping and using her own life force to make up for what the sword couldn't provide. She poured every fiber of her being into the flame.

"Still nothing?!"

The ball of fire was nearly seven feet wide and still filling up with energy when Earnest glanced up at the king's seat.

*Still? Hurry up... I can't hold out...*

...And then Blade's right arm swung down. She'd seen it.

*Finally! You idiot! Ugh! I trusted you, you know!*

"You're so *laaaaate*!"

With an ear-rending shout, Earnest brought down her sword.

The massive fireball plunged downward. The gigantic monster had her wings open, bare skin exposed as she began flapping—and the fireball exploded right into her. The flames burned her wings, tearing one of them apart.

Cú lost her balance in midair, tilting to one side as she tumbled back into the hole. There she lay, on her back, her underbelly—the place where a dragon's armor was thinnest—exposed to attack.

"Sophie!"

Earnest shouted down into the hole. Sophie, who had fallen in with Cú when the ground caved in, would be sure to hear, assuming she was still safe.

A blue flash erupted from below, piercing the air as it zoomed upward. Sophie's power—that power Earnest had called "unfair," and which Blade called "artificial hero force"—let her rewrite the laws of physics to her liking. It exhausted her to the core every time she used it, so she hadn't been able to practice this move in advance. But she didn't need to. All she was doing was hyper-strengthening the pull of gravity around her, locking Cú in place with her stomach exposed. Not even the dragon could overcome a force several hundred times her body weight pushing down on her.

The time limit was ten seconds.

"Earnest!" Blade's voice rang out.

Earnest stood up, leaning on her sword for support. That fireball just now had literally drained her strength. She was more weak than exhausted, and her body quivered. Nevertheless, she was still Earnest Flaming. She readied her sword, holding it high above her head.

"In the name of Earnest Flaming, I command you! Sword of mine, show me your powers!"

*"Wait. I, I can't—"*

"Shut the hell *up*!!"

A new fireball formed, one that blazed far hotter than her previous strike. It was even bigger than the one she drained herself to create just moments ago. It was simply incomparable, far wider than seven feet. She was practically creating a miniature sun. It was a good ten yards in diameter. No human being would have the energy to produce that alone—no, she could only manage it thanks to the many people placing their palms on her body.

"Anna! You can do it!"

"Come on, Empress!"

"Accept my strength, milady."

All their power streamed into her. Earnest howled, her entire body glowing gold.

*"Hraaaaaaaaaaaaah!"*

Five more seconds!

※

"Phew! That's some impressive force. To think a student of mine has achieved so much already…"

The king voiced his admiration between handfuls of chips. Once the fight reached its climax, he shooed his attendants away and focused on the action.

"She's not alone." Blade smiled slightly.

Taking the king by surprise made him feel a little triumphant. The way that half-eaten chip fell from his mouth spoke volumes.

A dozen or so lines of energy were pouring into Earnest. The students were linked together, forming a grid that the energy flowed through. Not many students could fully channel their energy like this, especially in a way that let them tap into their inner fighting force. Those that couldn't acted as "hubs," working that energy into a higher form, such as spirit, magic, or fighting force—whatever was necessary—and relaying it to its target.

Fifty or so students were still in the arena, and now all of their energy was gathering together in one place. In the end, it formed three thick lines—one for magic, one for spirit, one for fighting force—that connected straight to Earnest. This, she channeled directly into Asmodeus, allowing her to form that impressive fireball, an impossible feat for any one person.

*Cú. My daughter. Sit back and watch. This is what people can do.*

The fireball was now around twenty yards wide, big enough to almost reach the Proving Ground's ceiling. This was a force strong enough to outstrip a dragon's armored hide.

Cú still couldn't move, kept down by hyper-gravity. The effect of Sophie's artificial Hero force was set to expire in three, two, one—

Cú lay on her back with tears in her eyes…or, at least, it seemed that way to Blade.

"Let's *goooooooo*!!" With a shout, Earnest threw the giant ball of fire into the pit. It struck where Cú's armor was thinnest, then exploded.

*"Arrrrrgh! Arrrrrgh! Arrrrrgh!"*

Crying echoed across the Proving Ground. It was the dragon's way of indicating surrender.

## ○ Scene XV: End of the Battle

The battle was over.

Cú, now back in human form, was lying on the ground, her legs splayed out. Frankly, she was a mess, scratched and bruised from head to toe and covered in soot. Bits of her hair had burned as well.

Her opponents weren't in much better shape. Their faces were blackened;

all were about to collapse from exhaustion. Almost none of them could remain upright on their own, either leaning on supports or each other to stay standing. Lines of people formed, each one supporting the shoulders of their neighbor.

Only Earnest required no help to stay upright. She was Earnest Flaming, after all. Her spiritual force and pride alone were enough to do the trick.

"Was this all part of your calculations?" The king, standing next to Blade, whispered into his ear.

Blade brushed him aside with a hand. He hadn't calculated this at all—you couldn't really. Adults were *such* a pain to deal with.

There was no longer any real difference between the junior and senior classes. Before, there was a kind of unseen wall between the two—cleanly dividing the student body. Now, after fighting hand in hand, all of that was gone. They were all friends here.

Blade walked over to Cú, who was sitting, forlorn.

"Cú?" He tousled her hair.

"…I have lost," she said.

"Yeah."

"I have disappointed you, honored Father." She looked sadly up at Blade. "…Weak children get thrown away, don't they?"

"I'd never do that." He ran his hand around the top of Cú's head. "All you did was make one mistake. You're not weak at all. It was the people who were *strong*."

Cú looked at Blade, puzzled. After a few seconds, understanding erupted on her face.

"People are stronger than you," he said. "What do you think? Will you accept that now?"

"Yes." Cú nodded, looking refreshed.

"Okay. So you'll be friends with them, right?" Another pat on the head.

Everybody waited, all fifty or so of the soot-covered survivors and the other forty-odd wounded behind them. Even the most seriously hurt were now healed to the point where they could stand up. All of them were looking at Cú's face, waiting for her to speak.

"If…that's how it is, then, well, I don't mind being friends with you all. I am a broad-minded—"

"Uh-uh." Blade gave a light *bap* to the top of her head.

Cú took a deep breath, closing her eyes tight…and then she shouted.

"*Please* be my friends!"

"Of course!" a hundred and eight people shouted back.

# Epilogue

It was a typical afternoon in their usual dining hall.

"Wow. Katsu curry *again*?" asked Earnest critically.

"It's so good. *So* good. I love it."

Earnest was always nagging Blade about his food choices. She should just try some. Then she'd realize how much of a goddamn genius whoever invented it was.

"You have some curry on your face, Blade." Sophie reached out her hand and wiped Blade's lips.

He was bound to get more curry on his face in no time, but for some reason, Sophie kept on wiping it for him. She even had a Blade-specific napkin and everything.

"You don't have to spoil him like that, Sophie. Also, don't let him leave his vegetables. He never eats them otherwise."

"All right. Cú? Here, Cú. Say ahhh…" Claire brought a spoon to Cú's face.

"Oooh… I can eat by myself…," the dragon responded peevishly.

Despite her fretting, Cú was now much friendlier toward the others. She had accepted humans as a strong race, and now she was eager to spend time with anyone she met, creating some fatherly anxiety for Blade.

Incidentally, she didn't like the type of person who patted their lap and said, "Here, here, come on up," like Claire. She preferred to climb on people like Yessica and Kassim who weren't as eager to give her attention.

"Aw, don't say that. Okay? C'mon. Right here. Here!"

Claire was slapping her knee at that very moment, inviting Cú over. Cú reluctantly obeyed.

"Come on, Sophie. You gotta make him eat that side salad." Earnest was saying almost exactly what the lunch lady had told Blade earlier.

"Anna, if you want him to eat his veggies that much, why don't you just do *that*?"

"Come on, say *ahhh*..."

"...Ahhh."

Claire, in a very motherly gesture, brought a spoon up to Cú's lips. Cú, looking uncomfortable but not entirely opposed, opened up her mouth.

"Huh? No, no, no, no way! I'd rather die! ...No! Shut up! Be silent!"

Earnest paused mid rant to bash her sword on the floor a few times. Blade resolved to ask her what kind of witty repartee she was receiving from it these days.

"Blade? Your mouth." Sophie reached out her hand and wiped his lips.

"Oh, look at you! Spoiling him again! You need to stop that. He needs more discipline! If you give a man an inch, he'll take a mile, you know..."

"I'm fine with spoiling him. You can be his taskmaster for me, Earnest."

"Huh? Me? ...Why do *you* get to spoil him?!"

Blade turned his face away from the two of them and scanned the dining hall. A few students were staring at his table and snickering—some boys, some girls. They didn't bother averting their eyes when he looked at them, simply grinning amicably back. Blade smiled.

*Wow... I guess, if you put your mind to it...you really* can *make a hundred friends, huh?*

# Afterword

Hello, this is Shin Araki—and this is my first book for the Shueisha DASH X Bunko label. I've written books for a whole bunch of labels, but this time DASH X Bunko approached me with an offer, and so I'm launching this new series as part of the label's revamped lineup.

A manga version of *Classroom for Heroes* is being published in Shueisha's *Ultra Jump* magazine at the same time as this novel series. It's identical to the novels story-wise, kicking off with the chapter about Earnest— nicknamed the "red girl" by editorial. That being said, manga and text are two different storytelling methods, so they're bound to look and feel very different from each other. I encourage you to check out both!

By the way, just so you know, I am really bad at writing afterwords. I mean, I've already done my PR tour for this series, so I've run out of things to say. And I'm not even finished with the first page! They asked me for five! What'll I do? What'll I *dooo*?!

…But guess what! I've crafted the ultimate solution for a problem like this. I'll just break down the novel for you! If I do that, I'm sure that'll fill the pages in no time! I am *so* smart!

So here we go.

As you can see, the story is set in a fantasy world, one with Heroes and

Overlords. The humans that live on a green, bountiful continent are in conflict with a group of monsters that live in harsh conditions underground. They've been fighting for hundreds, maybe thousands of years. But right now, there's no Hero or Overlord, so the major hostilities have ended and there's a temporary peace.

This kingdom is occupied by true humans, as well as beings like elves, centaurs, and other demilings. Among them are so-called "champions," people with huge innate talents or who undergo insane amounts of training to gain crazy stats. How crazy are we talking? It's like one of those video games where one guy takes on hordes and hordes of foes. Blade, the main character, was raised among people like that, so his sense of what's normal is way off-kilter.

The technological level of this world is somewhere in the pre-Industrial Revolution phase. Magical engineering, however, has advanced greatly, so it's perfectly normal to see airships flying around, and there are even things akin to refrigerators and cooking stoves. They run on magic, however, so they're beyond the purchasing power of most people—you'd see them only in businesses and the homes of the very rich.

Volume 1 of this series features nothing but weapon-based combat, but magic is something that very much exists. Magic casters in battle are treated like large-scale cannons or artillery, and just one of them can turn the tide of a conflict. Still, soldiers with weapons form the core of any fight. In a world without large-scale weaponry like planes or tanks, close-range infantry combat is still the main trend.

Why aren't there planes and tanks, you ask? Well, because there are dragons, of course, both flying and nonflying. Primitive weaponry like that can't help you at all against such large monsters, so there's no reason for them to be invented in this world. That's also why you don't see small arms like guns or bazookas, either. With Heroes and champions milling around, it's a lot faster to go in slashing than to try firing a weapon. The best of them can also cast Dragon Eater, remember.

So that's how the tech level is on the surface…but underground, things have advanced a little further. So-called lost technology has been passed down by a certain cult from ancient times. This technology allows them to do things like clone people, raise the dead, create Guardians that can run forever... Nothing is impossible, really. The artificial Hero force that was key to the blue girl's—sorry, Sophie's—chapter in this book is driven by some lost tech like that.

That is the basic setting I've gone with. As for whether I'll have a chance to show off more of it in the future, well, it's hard to say right now. The plan is for *Classroom for Heroes* to be more character-driven. I'm putting the spotlight on this overpowered ex-Hero enjoying the peaceful second chapter of his life, and I'll be depicting how he teams up with the rest of the cast to solve his problems.

That's the direction we'll go in Volume 2 and beyond. Serious plot developments? Probably not gonna happen. Life-and-death battles? Also unlikely. A super-being tripping flags everywhere he goes? You can count on it.

Earnest, the red heroine...
Sophie, the blue heroine...
Cú, the yellow heroine...

I've introduced all three of them in this book. Did you find one that you like in particular?

By the way, in terms of their relations to Blade, Earnest is like his girlfriend (but not his lover), Sophie is probably his "mother," and Cú is his beloved daughter. Basically, it's the story of a man who's led a broken life but strives to regain his humanity. He had nothing as a Hero, but as the story progresses, he gains a girlfriend, then a mother, and finally a daughter. This is that kind of story.

Wow, is it me, or did that sound really good?!
I'm just about at five pages. The afterword's filled in! Perfect!

# About the author

**Shin Araki**

A character-oriented novelist who's done all kinds of work in the light novel industry. His love for characters outclasses everyone else's. He's also an expert at talking to himself.

**Illustrator: Haruyuki Morisawa**

A Tokyo-based illustrator from Toyama Prefecture. This is my first fantasy series in a while, so I'll give it my all!